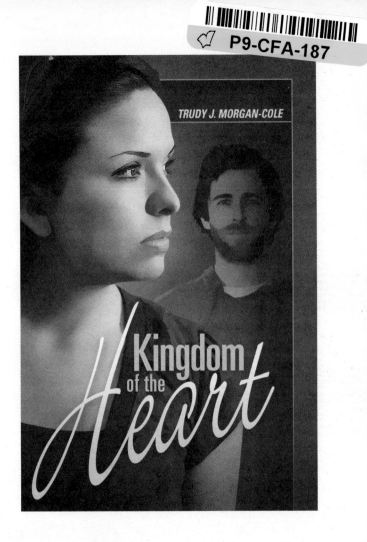

TRUDY J. MORGAN-COLE

Kingdom
of the
Heart

Pacific Press®
Publishing Association

Nampa, Idaho | Oshawa, Ontario, Canada
www.pacificpress.com

Cover design by Gerald Lee Monks
Cover design resources from iStockphoto.com
Inside design by Kristin Hansen-Mellish

The author assumes full responsibility for the accuracy of all facts and quotations as cited in this book.

Scripture quotations marked NIV are from the HOLY BIBLE, NEW INTER-NATIONAL VERSION®. Copyright © 1973, 1978, 1984 by International Bible Society. Used by permission of Zondervan Publishing House. All rights reserved.

You can obtain additional copies of this book by calling toll-free 1-800-765-6955 or by visiting http://www.adventistbookcenter.com.

Library of Congress Cataloging-in-Publication Data:

Morgan-Cole, Trudy J., 1965-
  Kingdom of the heart / by Trudy J. Morgan-Cole.
     pages cm
  ISBN 13: 978-0-8163-5023-0 (pbk.)
  ISBN 10: 0-8163-5023-X (pbk.)
1. Jesus Christ. 2. Christian. I. Title.
  PS3613.O7487K56 2014
  813'.6—dc23

                                    2014022253

June 2014

Table of Contents

Introduction

Some people think the most important question is, What would Jesus do? But an equally important one is, What will I do when I'm confronted with Jesus?

Christianity teaches that the Son of God lived as a human being in the Roman province of Judea about two thousand years ago. Jesus lived among ordinary people who spent time with Him, learned from Him, and had their lives turned upside down by Him.

Jesus came to a culture very different from our own, and it's important to understand those differences when we read His story in the Bible. But it's also important to remember that within the world in which they lived, those people who knew Jesus lived lives just as real to them as our lives are to us. They worked hard and raised their families. They worried about their fishing boats and their flocks and their farms the way we worry about our mortgages and our jobs being downsized.

When Jesus asked them to leave those things behind and follow Him, it was just as much of an upheaval for them as it would be for us.

This book tries to imagine Jesus coming not to the Middle

East in the first century but to a North American town in the twenty-first century. The things Chris Davidson says and does in these pages are based on the things Jesus said and did in the Gospels. And the people whose stories fill these pages are modeled on the characters that appear in the Bible story—not stained-glass saints but people as real as those we meet on the street every day.

This story asks every reader to face this question: If Jesus walked down the main street of my town, how would I respond to Him? And the follow-up question, How do I respond to His call in my life today?

The full-length version of *Kingdom of the Heart* will be available soon in print and eBook. Learn more about the story of Jesus in your favorite version of the Bible, or read *The Desire of Ages,* available at www.adventistbookcenter.com.

Chapter One

The grimy Coca-Cola clock on the wall of Pete's Garage showed 5:30. Pete wiped his hands on a utility rag, threw it aside, and grabbed his jacket off a peg on the wall. His brother Andy was just closing up the garage when a green Honda hatchback coughed, sputtered, and died in front of the garage doors. Pete shrugged and shook his head at the driver, but Andy flashed a smile at the harried-looking young woman who slipped out of the car.

Pete shook his head. "For heaven's sake, Andy," he muttered under his breath as he crossed the parking lot, "can't you just tell a customer we're closed?"

Even as the harried woman talked, Andy looked relaxed. His smile usually put people at ease, but this customer was too wound up to notice. She had a kid straddling her hip and another one clinging to her leg.

"It can't be the gas filter, can it? That's what was wrong with it the last time. My friend told me I should bring it here, but it's just luck I came here this time; you were the closest place . . ."

"No, ma'am, gas filter wouldn't make 'er stall that way. Too bad it's not; I could fix it for you right now."

Pete ground his teeth while Andy explained that he would have to buy the part from the Honda dealer, which couldn't be done sooner than tomorrow.

"But I'm desperate!" the woman whimpered. "I can't take the bus home with two kids, can I?"

"Listen, lady," said Pete. "You're lucky we even looked at your car, 'cause we're closed. See the sign? Now my brother here likes to be the Boy Scout and do his good deed for the day, but that part's not available till tomorrow!"

"I'm really sorry," Andy said.

One of the kids started to cry.

"I got no way home . . ."

"How far do you have to go?" Andy asked.

"Division Street and Birch."

An awkward pause. "Oh, what the . . . It's not too far out of our way, we'll drive you. Hurry up, we're late already." Pete was, as always, surprised to hear his own voice making the offer.

Driving back from the dingy row houses on Division Street, Pete and Andy got snarled in the six o'clock traffic jam. Pete swore softly and regularly, cursing the sun in his eyes, the other drivers, and the woman with the whiny kids. Andy hummed along with the radio. A smile twitched the corners of his mouth.

"What's so funny?"

"You are."

"Me?"

"First you rip a strip off that poor woman, then you go half-way across town to drive her home."

"Her and her screaming brats, who probably kicked a hole in the upholstery back there." Pete made no attempt to defend his contradictory behavior.

He thought of that again when they walked into the house and he dropped his jacket onto the floor. "What kind of man,"

Audrey was fond of saying, "at thirty-six years old still wears his high school jacket?" She hung it up—as she would again later tonight and had every night for fifteen years—with a shake of her head.

Pete wouldn't have parted with that jacket for diamonds. It had the Marselles Central High crest on the front, the team name, "Raiders," emblazoned across the back, and the words "Captain" and "Rocky" on the sleeves. He'd come a long way since Marselles Central High, but he was still proud of that jacket. And Audrey—a screaming, short-skirted freshman girl in the bleachers . . .

Audrey, he supposed, was currently an annoyed housewife in the kitchen. He rushed in to assure her he didn't mind eating a cold supper. But his plate was already in the microwave, and Audrey was laughing along with Andy at the story of their errand of mercy. Pete brushed his wife a quick kiss on the cheek, but she caught him around the waist and kissed him firmly on the lips.

Jenny was at the table, dawdling over a piece of cake. Pete sat down next to her. "Hi, angel, what's up?" The screen door burst open as Randy and Kevin tumbled over each other and into the kitchen.

"Daddy! Uncle Andy! Look!"

"I got a blue ribbon in the track meet! That's first place!"

The tangle of children swallowed up Pete. Audrey slid his dinner out of the microwave and placed it before him. Andy slipped his own plate into the oven. Pete dug his fork into a pile of mashed potatoes.

Pete Johnson. One lucky guy. And he knew it.

Chapter Two

Marie pulled up her chair to the cluttered dresser and switched on the lights surrounding the makeup mirror. Dusk was clouding the sky. Time to go to work. She began to smooth foundation over her still-silky skin, careful to use upward strokes. This kind of life aged girls fast: she must zealously guard against every wrinkle.

A soft cry came from behind the closed door. Shirley was having another of those nightmares that haunted her. To be like Shirley—now that was something to be avoided at all costs. She was twenty-three, five years younger than Marie, but she looked easily ten years older. It was the drugs mostly, of course, no question about that. Marie drank—more than she should if she hoped to keep her looks—and smoked marijuana, but she had stayed off the hard stuff so far.

She wriggled into her skirt, buttoned her blouse, and pulled on her jacket. A final touch of the brush to her cloud of black hair, and she was out the door, high heels teetering on the dingy narrow staircase.

The shortest way to Ellesmere Avenue, the nightclub strip where girls like Marie headed as twilight seeped through town, was past the hospital. Shirley always avoided it; she couldn't bear the stares of the well-heeled neighborhood people around Mercy General, the perfectly coiffured doctors' wives who sat on committees begging City Council to "clean up Ellesmere Avenue." Marie, on the other hand, took a perverse pleasure in walking past the hospital parking lot as the elegant matrons left the Auxiliary meetings, knowing that, in some cases, she knew their wealthy and powerful husbands as well as they did.

It can't go on forever, Marie reminded herself as she turned the corner and saw the lights of Ellesmere Avenue blinking in the distance. She was staying away from hard drugs and too much booze and keeping herself healthy for a reason. Someday she'd leave behind Ellesmere Avenue and this whole shoddy town. In a plush hotel in New York City, she'd be sought after by rich and important men. Maybe one of them would set her up in a fancy apartment, buy her a car and designer clothes and jewelry. Maybe, someday, love her. . . .

As soon as the forbidden word flitted through her mind, the blinds automatically snapped down behind her eyes and across a corner of her mind. Safe, stone-cold, hopeless as night, Marie strutted onto Ellesmere Avenue, lit a cigarette, and waited.

Chapter Three

"Perfect shot," Pete said as the dart hit its target.

James Fisher allowed himself a rare smile. "Now, if only you were as good at playing darts as you are at shooting pool, I'd have some competition!"

"Yeah, and if you were as good at running a business as you are at playing darts, I'd have some competition." Pete set down his glass and picked up a dart thoughtfully.

"It's no good criticizing me, ol' buddy, unless you're going to tell me what's wrong. What's the secret of success I'm missing out on?"

Pete let the dart fly before he turned to face James. "Aw, don't gimme that, Jim. You know what's wrong with your business and so does everyone else in this joint."

"Oh yeah?" James clenched his fists, set his jaw, and leaned forward, ready to take a swing. Their buddy Nat slapped him on the shoulder and said, "Take it easy," then had to dodge a swipe.

"Gotta give it to ya straight, Jim," Pete continued. "When a customer disagrees with you over a bill, you don't punch him out. When a car acts up, you don't break off the antenna. You pull a few stunts like that, word gets around. You lose business."

James's younger brother John was ignoring his brother and all his surroundings. Pete wondered why he was even here tonight. Normally, he avoided James's friends, and hangouts like Ranger's Bar. Most evenings John would be at a trendy downtown pub or else off to the library. He read constantly, silently smoldering in his fury at not being able to afford university.

The guys had calmed Jim down a bit, and now Nat glanced at his watch. "Time to head back home," he said. "You need a ride, Pete?"

"Not tonight. Audrey's got the kids out shopping for school clothes."

"Where's Andy tonight?" James asked.

Pete shrugged. "Am I my brother's keeper?"

"I sure wish I wasn't," James said, with a sidelong glance at John.

John's sullen face was suddenly animated. "Oh, right. You're the brother's keeper? You think I'm in this hick hole because this is where I like hanging out? I like the country music or something? I'm burning my brain cells out here because Mom told me she wants my precious big brother home early tonight—not drunk and not beat up! So you can just shut up about—"

With the speed of those practiced in their art, Pete and Phil moved to hold the brothers off each other. Pete was relieved to see Andy stroll through the door a few minutes later. His easygoing kid brother got along with everyone, and when he walked into the room the mood changed.

Tonight, though, an uncharacteristic urgency marked Andy's glance as he looked around at his brother and friends.

"Pete! You've got to come with me. I've met this amazing guy down on Lancer Avenue. He's a street preacher, and, man, he's amazing. Couldn't believe the stuff he was saying—and doing. You've gotta meet him!"

"Wait a second," said Phil, Nat's best friend and business partner. "I know the guy you're talking about. Drives a blue van and works with ghetto kids, right? I met him last week at a house where I was doing a job. Remember, Nat? I told you that you had to meet this guy. Chris Davidson, right?"

James waved his hand in dismissal. "A preacher? If you're into that kind of thing, send a few bucks to a charity and ease your conscience, but leave me out of it."

Maybe it was just the opportunity to disagree with James, but John suddenly looked interested, even eager. It was one of the few times Pete could remember such a look on his face. "I've heard of this guy too," John said, rising. "He sounds like a real radical. I want to meet him."

Half an hour later, Pete and Andy emerged from Phil's truck in front of the Lancer Avenue Community Center as James and John's car clattered to a halt behind them.

Pete had seen the place before—it was always dark and empty, broken windows boarded up, paint peeling off the sign. The brave community-improvement schemes of a more liberal age had faded under lack of funding and lack of commitment. Tonight, though, lights were blazing out of the few intact windows. A buzz of voices greeted them as they pushed the doors open.

In a large open room that looked like a high school gym, about forty or fifty people milled about. Two women came toward them—one was large and dark-skinned, the other small and Spanish-looking, Pete thought.

"Hi, I'm Erica," the African-American woman said. "You want to come in? You missed the meeting, but we'll be around for a few hours."

The other woman didn't seem as friendly. She frowned slightly. "You're not from around here, are you?"

Erica laughed. "They don't need no excuse to be here, Martha. People have been coming from all over town to see Chris."

Martha's tight face seemed to relax at the mention of the man's name. "He's been here all week, and the place has been packed every night."

The crowd in the middle of the room seemed to be breaking up; some leaving, others just dispersing. A lone man walked away, headed toward a group of children—then noticed the five men standing uncertainly and turned to them.

"Andy! You made it!" he called. "These your friends?" He was an average-looking guy, moderately tall, well-built but slim, dressed in jeans and a blue T-shirt.

Andy was making introductions. "I think you've met Phil—" he began.

"Sure!" Chris replied, shaking Phil's hand. "Fixing the sink in Hernandezes' apartment, right?"

"And looking for the contact lens," Phil added. He and Chris shared a laugh.

"Their teenage daughter wanted to know if her lens was anywhere in the pipes," Chris explained. "She'd lost it, oh, maybe six or seven months ago. Seriously, though, Phil, I was really impressed with the way you treated those people. They're so used to getting ripped off, and respect isn't something they see much of."

Phil looked at the ground and shrugged. "Satisfied customer's a repeat customer."

Chris Davidson turned to Pete. "Rocky Johnson. I've been waiting a long time to meet you." His handclasp was firm; no nonsense here. Pete glanced automatically at his sleeve for the telltale name tag—on the jacket he wasn't wearing.

"How'd you know to call me Rocky?" he blurted out.

Mr. Davidson smiled. "That's your name, isn't it? You still

think of yourself that way, and I do too. The Rock—someone you can build on and lean on. Some people call me that too. You're a born leader of men, Peter Johnson."

A shy-looking girl on crutches came up behind Chris and stood there, too hesitant to reach out and touch his sleeve. "Sir?" Andy said, and nodded toward the girl. But Chris was already turning around.

She beckoned him over, away from the men, and he bent to talk to her for a few moments. Pete looked at the other guys. No one seemed to have much to say. When the girl walked away, Pete noticed the happy, confident tilt of her head before he realized that her crutches were gone.

"He can do that?" Nat breathed.

"He can do anything," Andy said simply.

"It must be some kind of a trick . . ." suggested James.

"Shut up. This is no trick," Pete said roughly, not knowing where his certainty came from.

They stayed and watched him in action for another hour, talking to people, listening to them, healing them. Andy moved right into the crowd, helping out where he could, directing people to Chris. The others got involved more tentatively. Pete found himself in the Center's cramped kitchen, making a sandwich for a drunk and wondering, *What am I doing here?*

Back in his own kitchen later that night, Pete sat at the kitchen table looking at Audrey, at her hands moving in the little pool of light the lamp cast on the table. Her dark blond hair, pulled away from her face by a gold clip, shone a little in the light. Her fingers moved deftly on the keyboard of her laptop. "Paying bills," she explained, her eyes on the screen. "So, what happened tonight?"

"Audrey, I—we—met the most amazing guy." He tried to explain about Chris Davidson. "It would have been spooky," he finished, "him knowing our names and all that, but, it wasn't, see? It was just like—like he'd met us before."

"The way God knows us, I guess," Audrey said gently.

"He said I was—a leader of men. And I . . . Audrey, I'm just an average guy, right?"

She looked up from the computer, cupped her chin in her hands, and smiled. "No, honey. You're a bigmouth with a quick temper and a kind heart—both of which you usually keep hidden—and you have a lot of frustration bottled up inside because you've never found a challenge that will let you be the man you're meant to be."

"And now . . . I think I've found it," Pete said.

Audrey looked back down at the screen. "I'd like to meet this Mr. Davidson."

Chapter Four

Audrey tossed Pete a dish towel. Pete was slowly becoming a liberated husband, but not as slowly as he'd have liked. He took a cereal bowl out of the dishwasher and gazed out the kitchen window as he wiped it dry.

"You've been awfully quiet lately," Audrey observed. "Something on your mind?"

In fact, Pete had a lot on his mind. Weeks ago, Chris Davidson had asked Pete, Andy, and the rest of their group of friends to "follow him." Pete wasn't really clear on what that meant, but he knew it would mean leaving his job and possibly leaving home to join Chris's mission full time. He was making plans to turn the day-to-day operation of the garage over to Stan Carey, the other mechanic who worked there alongside Pete and Andy.

Pete had never even considered such a major career move without consulting Audrey. Ever since his bid for senior class president, eighteen years before, Audrey had been involved in his every decision. But now—how could he tell her he wanted to walk away from it all? She had enough worries with her sick mother staying in the house with them. The last thing she needed was to worry about Pete taking an extended leave from work. Even as Pete thought that, he knew it was a lame excuse for not telling her.

James and John were closing up shop too. An unexpected windfall had appeared in their business bank account—Pete was pretty sure Chris had had something to do with that. The Fisher boys had been able to pay off their debts and give their mother a little money. They were with Chris all the time now: working at the Center, gathering groups to listen to his street-corner sermons, and going with him to visit some of the scummiest neighborhoods of Marselles.

Pete knew himself to be impulsive. His immediate response to Chris's invitation had been "Yes! Of course I'll follow you!" Only as he made his way home did the question of Audrey and the kids drill into his vision-soaked brain.

Audrey sighed and closed the dishwasher door. "Forget it. I can see I'm not getting anything out of you this morning." Footsteps thundered on the stairs, and she raised her voice. "Are all of you ready for church?"

"I can't find my shoes!" Kevin yelled.

"He's got on my sweater, and I want to wear it!" Randy chimed in.

Churchgoing was a regular weekly ritual at the Johnsons'. Pete had never been all that religious, but as soon as Randy was born Audrey had insisted on weekly church attendance, and he'd complied. Lately, church had confused Pete. *With all the time I'm spending with Chris Davidson,* he thought, *I should be getting more religious. Instead, I'm getting impatient with church.*

"Chris is preaching today," Andy said as the whole family piled into the minivan on the way to church.

"He's what?"

"He's the guest speaker."

"That'll be nice," Audrey said placidly. "We should invite him back to our place for lunch."

"Nice is the one thing it won't be," Pete said grimly. "A disaster is what it'll be."

Pete felt no need to revise his prediction when Chris Davidson stood up behind the pulpit later that morning. Nobody else in the large congregation looked worried, though. They all knew him well by now—a few of them had even volunteered time down on Lancer Avenue. They described Chris Davidson as "interesting" or "challenging" or "intriguing" and settled back comfortably in their seats and hoped to hear an inspiring sermon about the need for social action.

Pete knew better.

The text he chose for Scripture reading was innocent enough—it seemed to fit in with what most of his hearers were expecting. "The Spirit of the Lord is on me, because he has anointed me to preach good news to the poor. He has sent me to proclaim freedom for the prisoners and recovery of sight for the blind, to release the oppressed, to proclaim the year of the Lord's favor."[1]

"Friends," Chris began in his clear, ringing voice, "we all know that this text tells us what God wants us to do in the world. But we also know it's much more than that: it's a prophecy about what God's Chosen One will do when He comes to save the world. You've all looked forward to His coming; all your lives you've heard sermons about how this world will change when God sends His special Messenger to lead you out of blindness and captivity and poverty. Well, I'm here to tell you that you don't need to wait any longer. That time is here! God's Chosen One is here! Today, in this church, this scripture is being fulfilled."

A low murmur ran around the edges of the congregation as Chris went on talking and the impact of his words sank in.

People leaned forward to catch what he said.

"The kingdom of Heaven—the kingdom of God—that perfect world of peace and goodwill that you've all been waiting for—it's not something far-off in the future. It's not a fantasy or a fairy tale. It's here now. If you choose to believe, this kingdom will begin right in your heart. It will begin here in Marselles, with all of you who choose to believe in the One sent by God."

Murmurs grew louder now. A few people got up to leave. A man across from Pete got to his feet and called out, "Just what are you trying to—" but was firmly yanked down by his wife.

Chris Davidson met the man's eyes. "What I'm trying to do is this—wake up the good people of Marselles and tell them a new day is coming. What I'm trying to say is that you can be a part of this new day—all of you—if you'll be willing to leave the safe lives you know, and believe me, and follow me." He stretched out his hands and looked out into the congregation for a moment, then turned quickly and sat down.

Back home, Audrey was concerned about getting dinner on the table as quickly as possible. The only way they'd managed to get Chris away from the mob scene in the parking lot was to tell everyone where he'd be in the afternoon. Audrey was afraid people—the angry, the eager, the curious—would start ringing the doorbell before her roast was even out of the oven.

Chris seemed more amused than worried by the response to his sermon. "I wish I'd gotten this much of a positive response when I preached that sermon in my hometown," he said with a smile on the way home from church.

When at last they were ready to sit down, though, Chris was nowhere to be seen. "I'll go find him!" volunteered Jenny, kicking back her chair and racing away from the table.

"No, me!" shouted Randy, tearing off after her.

A moment later, Randy reappeared in the doorway. "Mr.

Davidson was upstairs with Grandma," he announced solemnly. Down the hall behind him came Audrey's mother and Chris, with Jenny in between clinging to both their hands.

"Mom, what are you doing out of—" Audrey's sharp voice faded away. Pete looked at his mother-in-law and had the strange feeling of being caught in a time warp. This white-haired woman with the steady step and clear eyes was Ethel Delaney as he remembered her looking the day he married her daughter (though without the look of sorrowing disapproval she'd worn that day). She bore little resemblance to the frail, sickly woman of recent months.

"It's all right, dear," Ethel said in a firm voice. "I'm fine now. Mr. Davidson has healed me. Is there anything I can do to give you a hand?"

The family barely had time to marvel over Ethel's sudden recovery; the house was busy all afternoon and evening. Church people and neighbors dropped by to meet Chris Davidson and talk to him. Some tried to challenge him on what he'd said that morning, but Pete didn't hear any loud arguments.

It was late that evening when the crowd finally thinned. James and John and their mother were the last to leave, except for Chris himself, who sat in the lamp-lit kitchen with Jenny on his knee and Kevin beside him.

Pete hadn't had a moment to talk to Audrey all day. Now he came out onto the back deck where she sat alone. "Quite the day, wasn't it? You sure you didn't mind all those people here?"

"Well, how could I mind?" Audrey said. "They came to see Chris. After what he did for Mom, I wouldn't want to keep anyone from seeing him." She paused. "Pete?"

"Mmm-hmmm."

"Do you believe in Chris? I mean, do you believe he is who he says he is?"

Pete was quiet, too, looking out at the yard filled with toys the kids had played with earlier today. "It's really weird, but . . . yeah, I guess I do." Another pause. "What about you?"

Audrey nodded. "Believing he's the Son of God means I have to totally rearrange everything I've ever thought. He asked you and Andy to come with him, didn't he?"

"Well . . . he wants us to help him out. Full time, I guess."

"I had a long talk with Chris today," she went on. "He explained why he needs you, and how he asked you to give up everything to follow him."

"And?"

"Well, if I believe in him, I can't hold anything back, can I? I've enjoyed the security of your having the garage, but security's not everything."

Hesitantly, Pete admitted his plan to turn over the garage to Stan. "I'm sorry I didn't talk to you first."

"It's OK . . . I wish you'd trusted me enough to ask me about it, but I understand. Chris says he'll be going on the road for a while, maybe taking you and Andy and the other guys with him. Anyway, I was talking with some of the folks who volunteer down at the Center—Bob and Erica Washington, Martha Castillo, people like that. Not everyone can go on the road with Chris, but those of us who are left behind can keep doing his work here in Marselles after he leaves."

"You've really thought this through, haven't you?"

"It's the most important thing that'll ever happen in our lives." She got up and went over to a bag of garbage leaning in the corner of the deck and started picking up napkins and paper cups, dropping them into the bag. "Maybe in the summer, when the kids are out of school, we can drive to wherever you are and spend some time together."

"I'd like that," Pete said. He touched her cheek as she

straightened up, and covered his action by tucking back a stray wisp of her hair. Then he took the bag from her. "I'll carry this."

---

1. Luke 4:18, 19, NIV.

Chapter Five

"I understand why he had to leave, but it sure is different around here without him," Erica sighed. Down at the Community Center, Erica Washington was known as a pillar of strength and a source of good cheer. Here in Martha Castillo's kitchen, she just looked like a tired, middle-aged African-American woman, dressed in faded jeans and a flowered print blouse.

Her companion was a marked contrast. Martha Castillo, short, thin, and wiry, was younger than Erica, still a few years short of forty. Martha didn't allow herself the luxury of sitting at the table with her head in her hands. She worked while she talked, polishing the bottom of a copper pot in her cramped but spotless kitchen.

Martha had long ago steeled herself to expect nothing from life but simple duties and small pleasures. Until the appearance of this Chris Davidson person on Lancer Avenue, life had obligingly met her expectations. Now that he had gone, the disquieting element of hope could be put to rest too. She was disappointed, of course, but disappointment was the easiest emotion to deal with; it was the one she'd had the most practice at.

Of course, she said none of this to Erica. What she said was,

"Well, now that we've got people together, maybe we can work on City Hall to improve some things. There's that petition to get funding for the Center . . ."

Erica rubbed at a patch of the table's shiny surface. "Yeah, there's stuff like that, we got to keep that up, but . . . I don't know, when Chris was here it was more than just that. More than politics—there was a new spirit."

Martha edged away from the subject. It bordered on religion, and religion made her uneasy, except when it involved collecting clothes for the needy or putting on baked goods sales to raise funds for a new church roof. "Mr. Davidson certainly made a change in a lot of people," she conceded.

"Well, your brother, for instance," Erica pointed out.

Martha nodded shortly. The easiest way to annoy her was to mention Larry. His broad smile, his whistle, his easy stride, all made her hackles rise when she thought of all the trouble he'd caused her. "We'll just see how long that lasts, now," she told Erica.

"Oh, give him a chance. He's such a nice boy, and now that he has that good steady job, I'm sure he'll do all right."

"Yes, if it was the first time he had a good steady job." Martha put aside the pot and picked up another one to scrub.

Larry had been the family's hope. He fitted in neatly between his older sister and his younger, who were both so different and so difficult. While their widowed mother fretted over pretty Maria, whom boys wouldn't leave alone, and plain Martha, whom boys wouldn't notice, all three of the Castillo women had pinned their dreams on the tall, handsome charmer with the ready smile. He would grow up, go to college, get a good job, and move them all off Lancer Avenue.

"Poor Mom," Martha said aloud. "All three of us ended up being a worry to her in the end."

"Now, you couldn't have been much of a worry," Erica said. "You were such a big help to her."

"Yes, well, she worried I'd never get married. But I think in the end she was just as glad I didn't. Who else would there have been to care for her, after Maria nearly broke her heart and then she got so sick? Then Larry's wife left him and took the baby, and he came back home. Mom would never have died peacefully if she hadn't known there was someone to look after her boy. As it was, she didn't have a worry in the world when she died, except not knowing what happened to poor Maria. And I would have gladly spared her that trouble, if I could have."

"No, you couldn't do anything about that, could you now," Erica agreed. Her eyes strayed involuntarily to Maria's picture on the shelf, and Martha's gaze followed hers. Martha had often wanted to put the picture away, but Larry wouldn't hear of it. It showed Maria at thirteen, four years before she left home. Dark eyes peeked out from under a stylish tangle of dark curls. Her mouth was crooked up at one end into that teasing grin that drove Lancer Avenue boys wild.

After Erica had gone, Martha began to scrub the sink as if her brisk strokes could erase the memories that had been called up. All the while Chris was in Marselles, he had tried to talk to her alone. Larry spent long hours sitting out on the front step with him, but Martha avoided being alone with Chris as much as possible. Now it seemed that in his absence, he was forcing her to do what she'd not done in his presence—to go over the past, shaking out old memories she had long since folded and put away.

It had taken years of effort for Martha to look at that kitchen door without seeing Maria huddled there, crying and trembling; without hearing her own voice ordering Maria to get out of the house and never to show her face again. Larry would have stopped her, but he was newly married then and had moved out. And their mother was helpless, reduced to tears and disbelief. Seeing Mom like that was what drove Martha to rage . . . knowing that Maria, like Larry, could cause their mother so much heartache. Better to end all the hurt, to drive Maria out into the rainy night. Where had she gone? What had she done? Over the years, Martha had trained herself not to ask these questions, but tonight they echoed in every stroke of her scouring pad.

For once, Martha's hands were still at the kitchen sink. She stood there, her thin freckled arms braced and her head bent, until she heard Larry's key in the lock. But as her hands moved firmly back to their work, it was not her brother she longed to talk to, but Chris Davidson.

Chapter Six

Late afternoon sun slanted across the hills, filtered through trees just turning red and gold, and spilled across a dozen men sprawled on the ground. A battered blue van was parked in a nearby lot.

Pete put on his jacket. The air was getting nippy. They had just driven away from a small town where things had gone really well for a week or so, until some of the local clergy got a little upset by things Chris Davidson had said. The crowds liked Chris. They followed him around for days, listening to his sermons, bringing sick people to be healed—but then there had been some threats, and Chris had said it was time to move on. It was a familiar pattern by now.

Two summers and one long winter had passed since they had driven out of Marselles. Chris's original group of six men had grown to twelve core members, and they were a motley crew. The Marselles guys were bad enough. Pete had known his brother, the Fishers, Nat and Phil, for years, but he'd never envisioned roaming the country in a van with them for more than a year. The newcomers had made it even worse.

The college boys were probably the worst. Big, strapping,

successful-looking guys with college degrees—it annoyed Pete that mere kids could be so polished. Matt had turned out not to be so bad. He was pathetically happy to be anywhere near Chris and gladly took on the grubbiest jobs. His buddy Jude was another matter altogether. Smooth-talking and super-organized, he'd tagged along with them a few months after Matt showed up. He handled the money, the PR, the details of the organization.

Probably the member of the group who'd caused the most discomfort was Simon, the skinhead. Head shaven, stomping around in black jeans, a black shirt bearing the logo of some punk band, and vicious-looking Dr. Martens, Simon had been eyed warily by all of them at first. Thad, the only African-American member of the group, almost left when Simon showed up. To him, a white guy with a shaved head was a racist neo-Nazi. While Simon didn't appear openly bigoted, he also didn't make a point of saying he wasn't a White supremacist. Chris had talked to both men separately, and they'd both stayed, though hostility had simmered unspoken.

Where hostility *had* been spoken was between Simon and John. Pete was never too clear on the differences between all these radical young people. As far as he was concerned, John and Simon both dressed funny and got angry at "society" a lot. But, apparently, their philosophies were completely different, on top of which they liked different music, which seemed to be a bigger deal. Some of their fights had gotten pretty physical before Chris broke them up.

If Pete had to pick his own pet peeve, the least favorite of his traveling companions, it would have to be Tomas. Tomas was a tall, muscular Latino guy from down-in Texas somewhere, and Pete, on first seeing him, had assumed he was a migrant farm worker. So much for racial stereotypes. Tomas turned out to be a high-school science teacher with an unusually keen mind. Davidson's group was composed of a generous mix of educated and uneducated men, but Tomas was the only one who considered himself an intellectual and had the degree to prove it.

At first Pete and Tomas got along famously, because they shared a love for argument. They'd while away the hours on the road as they'd debate politics, religion, sports—anything. What Pete lacked in book learning and long words, he made up for in passionate conviction. Which was why Tomas eventually began to irk him. The man took no firm position on anything. He could switch sides in a debate without batting an eyelash. He questioned everything. It was inquiry itself he loved; he had no desire to find answers. Tomas wasn't sure he believed in God. Tomas didn't even support one particular ball team, though he could argue for hours about anyone's chances of winning the pennant.

Pete snapped out of his reverie to notice Phil getting up and walking away. He looked at the Fishers. "Where's Phil off to?" he asked.

Jim shrugged. "Probably gone to look for Nat."

"Yeah, Nat's been pretty down lately," John agreed.

"Well, no wonder! Look at the way his wife's been treating him—getting a legal separation and all that garbage! Sure, Sue was really supportive when he started out with Chris, but look what she's doing to him now. I don't know how he stands it!"

"Don't be too hard on her, Pete," Jim cautioned. "Not every woman's like Audrey, you know. I figure I couldn't do this if I was married—even with Mom, I think she's only putting up with it 'cause she knows Chris has got a pretty big future and we're going to be part of it."

"Is it really all worth it?" Pete wondered aloud. "I mean, we take off and leave our jobs, leave our families with no real security, and traipse all over the countryside, and what do we accomplish? Chris gets his name on the evening news and draws a few crowds, then some preacher or politician gets mad and we're on the road again. I mean, is it really going anywhere?"

"I think it is," James said. "Look at all the attention we're getting, nationwide. Jude says Chris could even run for Congress and win, probably, next election."

"Jude's full of it," said John.

"By the way, either of you seen Chris lately?" Pete interrupted. The diversion worked.

"No, but he's been gone for hours," John said. "I was just going to go look for him."

"I think I'll join you," said Pete, getting up. Jim fell in beside them.

One great thing about Chris Davidson was that you could never bother him. He had a lot to put up with, what with his powerful enemies and his contentious friends, and he often slipped away for some solitude. But if one or more of the guys strolled up while he was sitting alone, praying as he usually was, he never seemed annoyed.

And indeed, his smile was wide and welcoming when they saw him a few minutes later, walking toward them on a twisting path through the trees.

"Hi! I was just coming back to look for you guys." The four of them angled off together on another path that wound uphill.

"Where are you heading?" Pete asked.

Chris smiled. "Off to meet someone," he said, but didn't elaborate till they reached the top of the hill, when he said, "I came here to talk to the Father. I want you to join me." They knelt awkwardly in the grass, and Chris knelt a little farther off. Pete bowed his head to pray—an activity he'd done more of recently than in his whole past life—but Chris raised his face to the sky.

Pete's mind wouldn't stay on prayer. He was thinking how great it was to be up here alone with Chris, just the three of them and none of the others. Though Chris spent a lot of time alone with each of the men, he seemed to single Pete, James, and John out more often. Pete and Jim liked to rub this in a little with some of the other guys. It never hurt to remind them who Chris's closest friends were. John had caught them at this game one day and laughed himself silly.

"You guys are something else," he told Jim and Pete. "You really think Chris spends the most time with us 'cause we're the best? Get real, man! Who does he most often have to haul out of a fight? Who gives him the most headaches? Man, Chris Davidson takes time out for us 'cause we're the ones who need him the most!"

The memory of John's words made Pete squirm. *You're praying,* he reminded himself, when James whispered, "Look!"

Pete opened his eyes and wondered how he could have failed to notice how intense the light had grown. Looking toward the source, he saw Chris Davidson standing with a stranger on either side. The figures were familiar, like pictures in old Bibles, maybe. One was ancient and white-bearded, with flowing robes and a staff in hand. The other was clad in rough garments, with a visionary look in his glittering eyes.

"They—they look like—Moses and Elijah," John whispered.

The figures did not speak, but seemed to agree. Their faces beamed at the shocked men, who then turned toward Chris.

Chris Davidson—was this the same man who had changed a flat on the van that morning? Pete couldn't see the worn jeans and familiar T-shirt. Chris seemed to be clothed in light—light that glowed and shone from his body. His always vivid eyes glowed with a power not earthly. Beside him, Moses and Elijah in their beards and biblical robes looked positively ordinary.

Then the Voice came. It came from the sky and the ground; it burst from inside Pete's head and pressed on him from the air around. It was deep and commanding as only one Voice in all the universe could be, yet filled with a wild passion, a passion both of joy and sadness, of tenderness and steel.

"This is My Son, whom I love dearly. Listen to him!"

That was all the Voice said, but Peter Johnson knew he would never cease hearing it. His eyes were closed now, but the light still burned against them. He pressed his hand to his heart and felt it pounding. He touched his face and found it damp with streaming tears.

He was huddled on the ground, but a moment later he felt a tap on his shoulder and he heard Chris's voice saying, "Get up. Don't be afraid." Opening his eyes, he was surprised to see Jim and John on either side of him.

The light had faded. The echoes of the Voice had stilled; once again the wind blew and the birds chirped. Moses and Elijah had vanished without a trace. Chris stood alone in front of them. "Let's go down and find the others," he said.

He wore faded jeans and a blue T-shirt. His voice and his walk were familiar. His face seemed to glow, holding a hint of unearthly glory. But perhaps that had always been there? And he was still their best Friend, traveling Companion, their Chief. But perhaps, even in that moment of glory, he had never been anyone else.

Chapter Seven

Marie's shoulders ached as she walked, and the chilly wind numbed her fingers. She considered setting the grocery bags down for a moment, but knew that would only slow her. She'd just have to pick them up again, anyway.

When Marie was little and walking back from the grocery store, Mom would always give her the bag with the bread in it to carry, because that was light. She'd swing the bag in a wide arc as she skipped down the sidewalk. Martha, walking primly on the other side of Mom, would scold, "Don't do that, Maria, you'll break the bag."

Marie shifted her grip on the bag's plastic handles, which were cutting into her palms. She tried to bring her thoughts back to the present. It was a habit of hers to avoid all thoughts of childhood and family. But simple, homely activities, such as grocery shopping, sometimes brought back the past in a rush. Now she couldn't stop thinking of Martha, Mom, and Larry.

The family of four was evenly divided: Mom and Martha, hardworking and sensible, made up the dominant half; on the other side were Marie herself and Larry. He was the only one who understood her, who sympathized when she got into trouble at school or disobeyed Mom or Martha. Larry, too, liked a good time. He told her they must both take after their dad, though neither of them remembered him well.

Marie slowly climbed the steps to her apartment. The door was ajar and she could hear Shirley humming along with the radio. She shouldered the door open and staggered to the kitchen table, where with relief she dropped the bags.

Shirley, fixing Kraft Dinner for supper, was in a chatty mood. "What's the matter with you tonight, Marie? You're awful quiet."

"Ah, nothing. Well, I don't know, I was just thinking about my family."

"Oh yeah? What about them?"

"Oh, nothing." Marie kicked off her shoes and put her feet up. "It's stuffy in here, even though it's so cold outside."

Shirley tugged the window open. The yellowish curtains waved in the sudden breeze. She stuck an empty tin can under the window to prop it open. "Mostly I just forget I ever had a family," she said over her shoulder. "After all, they forgot I existed, why shouldn't I do the same?"

"Yeah," Marie agreed. "I mostly forget my family too. My sister threw me out of the house when I got pregnant."

"No kidding?" Shirley said. "Isn't it strange we've lived together so long and we don't really know anything about each other's past?"

Marie remembered meeting Simon at a party when she was fifteen, brave enough by then to defy her mother, her disapproving sister, her protective big brother. Anyway, Larry's reputation, a thing to be feared on Lancer Avenue, meant nothing to Simon Noble. Simon wasn't from their neighborhood: he went to St. Vincent's, uptown, and lived in Westchester Park. Larry Castillo didn't exist in Simon Noble's world. But Maria Castillo did. Very much so.

Yes, Simon was a good memory, for a while. Marie had been really proud that Simon wasn't ashamed to openly acknowledge her as his girlfriend. He took her to Westchester Park parties where she was never properly dressed but always made a hit anyway. Marie knew she'd found real love with Simon, who treated her like a princess. Her mother's and Martha's lectures had always been easy to ignore. But even Larry's dire warnings about men fell completely under the force of her love for Simon.

Marie took a last long drag on her cigarette and stubbed it out fiercely in the ashtray. But memory, once lit, was not so easily extinguished. Shirley scraped the macaroni out onto plates and sat down across from her. "So you got pregnant and left home," Shirley probed. "What happened?"

The question called forth all the images Maria was trying to keep back. Reluctantly, she said, "It's no big story. I told my mom and sister, because I figured, well, my brother got his girlfriend pregnant and it was no big deal, they just got married and that was it. But when I told them I was pregnant? The place blew up! My mom locked herself in the bedroom and my sister told me to leave and never come back." Words, so stark and simple, disguised the voices and tears and pain that time couldn't erase. "So I left. I went to see my boyfriend. We'd been going out a long time so I figured he'd probably marry me."

"Ha! Bet you got a surprise."

"Oh yeah. He dropped me like a hot potato. His family was real rich, and I guess he didn't want to hit them with a big scandal, you know? He did give me some money. I was mad, of course. I didn't want to take his money, but I was pretty desperate too. So I used the money to get out of town." The pain was tearing at her chest now. Maybe Shirley would be content, would stop asking questions.

"So you came here?"

"Uh huh."

"And what happened—you know—did you have the baby?"

"Shirl, why am I telling you this? I never talk about this. Look, I got here and I had an abortion. End of story."

Shirley's face softened. "Oh yeah, I had one when I was sixteen. It's rough. I'm sorry."

Marie closed her eyes and drew a new cigarette to her lips. "So there was this guy I met when I moved here, and I lived with him for a while. He loaned me the money for the abortion, when I got well again I had to pay him back, and there was only one way I could make money, so I went out on the street for him."

"Oh, that's awful." Marie could see Shirley just itching to tell her own life story. No. Not tonight. Enough of her own memories; she couldn't carry someone else's too. She stood up. "Well, Shirl, I've got to go to work—thanks for supper. You going out tonight?"

"Yeah, later. See ya."

Ellesmere Avenue was slow tonight. Marie knew why. That religious dude was in town, preaching in the park and getting everybody worked up. Some people didn't like him, but an awful lot went out to hear him. Not only was this religious kick bad for business tonight, Marie knew it would lead to another round of crackdowns and arrests in the next few weeks. The good citizens would be eager to clean up the town—at least temporarily.

No cars slowed down, no one strolled up to her. It was a cold night. Marie pulled her jacket around her and shivered. How much longer? When she spotted a lone man walking down the street toward her, she decided it was time to take a risk. Normally, she waited for customers to approach her; to approach them was soliciting, and that was asking for trouble with the cops. But tonight she needed the money, and she felt lucky.

Not lucky enough. When the man made eye contact with her but didn't walk over, she called out to him softly. He listened to her offer, came a little closer . . . and pulled out his badge.

Marie said nothing in the police cruiser on the way to the station. She had never been picked up before, and she was scared. Normally, the penalties were light enough, but now, with this sudden tide of morality sweeping the town, they might choose to make an example of her.

A crowd thronged the square outside the building that held the town hall, courthouse, and police station. The floodlights were switched on.

"Is that guy still out here?" one cop asked the other.

"You kidding? Does he ever go home? He's been out here preaching all day, and there's been a crowd like this the whole time. We had to have guys out there round the clock, crowd control, you know?"

They both held Marie's arms as they led her out of the car and up the steps, their hands brushing her body. She hated cops—hated the fact that in their eyes the same greedy lust she was used to seeing in her clients was coupled with righteous indignation. *Pigs,* she thought.

As they jostled through the edges of the crowd, Maria overheard snatches of conversation. About the preacher, no doubt.

"You can say what you like, but look, he healed my kid."

"It all sounds great now, but this isn't good for the town. People will—"

"I've never heard anyone talk like him! Is it true that he—?"

One shrill voice rose above the rest. "That's the kind of thing he ought to be concerned about!"

Marie's escorts stopped, and Marie looked around with a sinking feeling. She saw the smooth blond head of Mrs. Denver, wife of the head surgeon at Mercy General, saw Mrs. Denver's beautifully manicured fingers pointing at her. The shrill voice had attracted some hearers. "It's all well and good for Mr. Davidson to talk about the kingdom of heaven and tell us to clean up our act, but if he's really concerned about morality, he ought to have something to say about this kind of thing!"

This kind of thing, also known as Marie, felt her heart racing beneath her scratchy lace blouse. Voices joined in with Mrs. Denver's, "Let's see what he does have to say."

"This should be fun," one of Marie's cops said to the other, over her head. Mrs. Denver was ascending the steps. Her red-nailed fingers tore Marie's arm out of one policeman's grip. Head held high, she charged back down the stairs, dragging Marie and the other policeman behind her. The cop caught her crusading spirit, and he and Mrs. Denver elbowed through the crowd so forcefully that Marie stumbled, half-running, trying to keep up.

This would be funny, Marie thought, *if it weren't so scary.* She did not want to meet this man. With ordinary men, she always counted on their desire to temper their disapproval. But she'd seen ministers and religious fanatics before. They were far worse than cops. The lust was there, all right, but they felt so guilty for it that they covered it up with passionate hatred. She understood why in olden days these men—these holy men—used to whip and even stone prostitutes, why in some countries they still did it. She'd seen the fire in their eyes.

Then the crowd parted, and she caught a quick glimpse of a man in front of her before Mrs. Denver and the cop—aided by a few people behind them—pushed her forward. She fell onto her hands and knees—holes in her stockings, gritty stones drawing blood—and stayed there, fighting back sobs. Above, she could hear them challenging him, asking what should be done with her.

She became aware that he was no longer towering over her. She looked up to see him crouched in front of her, looking steadily at her. She glanced up at the ring of solid citizens around them, illuminated by the floodlights' glare. Marie's eyes were driven away from their cold stares, but she could not meet his eyes, either.

"Maria."

It was just a whisper—her name. Her old name, her childhood name. It drew her eyes up to his. At first she couldn't understand what was missing in his gaze. Then she knew. Though his face seemed to promise kindness and concern, there was no hint of lust there. He was seeing her not as a beautiful woman but as a human being. Other men's eyes had undressed her body; this one bypassed it to undress her soul. She cringed, but could not turn away.

He looked away, up at the spectators. His voice was clear, with a sharp note in it. "Perhaps," he said slowly, "whoever is perfectly innocent here ought to step forward and condemn her."

Utter silence. Marie kept her eyes on the preacher, but he still looked at the eyes of the crowd, as if challenging someone to step forward.

Then he looked down at the ground. With his finger, he began to trace patterns in the gravel and sand beside him. Curious, the onlookers strained to see. Marie could tell that he was not simply doodling, but writing. She could not pick out the words, but, apparently, someone in the crowd could. An exclamation broke the silence, and someone hurried away. A murmur ran round. Chris Davidson kept writing—it looked as though he was writing words, names, dates. Marie didn't take her eyes off him, but she dimly heard more feet shuffling away.

From behind, she heard one of the cops whisper, "I'm not

stickin' around to find out what he knows about me." Footsteps. More murmurs. Then quiet again.

Chris stopped writing and faced her again. He balanced on the balls of his feet, his large hands resting on his knees. He was smiling, half-amused, half-sad.

"Where are the people who are accusing you?" he asked. The smile on his lips and in his eyes had seeped into his voice. He looked around the square, and her gaze followed his. The ring of spectators was gone. She looked back at him and shook her head.

"You mean there's no one here to condemn you?"

"No one."

His smile broadened, and he stood up, then reached out his hands to pull her to her feet. When she stood in front of him, he kept hold of her hands. His face grew serious again.

"Then I don't condemn you either. You can go, Maria—but leave this life of sin behind."

Marie could say nothing. A chill wind blew across the square, but she hardly felt it. Still looking into his eyes, she dropped again to her knees before him. It was the only thing to do.

Chapter Eight

Pete shifted uncomfortably. He lay on his back, arms folded under his head. Beside him Audrey breathed deeply and steadily. *What a place for the wife and kids to have to come visit me!*

His eyes, adjusted to the irregular light cast by a flickering neon sign on the street outside, could see shadowed shapes all around—men, women, and children huddled on the floor. There must have been about forty people there, all told. The usual crowd of twelve, and some who were traveling with them—Audrey and the kids, a few of the other guys' families, Erica and Bob Washington from Marselles, people like that. And people they had just met today, who had stayed so late talking and listening to Chris Davidson that they just never bothered to return home.

The girl who had been at the center of that weird scene in front of City Hall tonight—she was here somewhere, sleeping on the floor. Or was she also lying awake? Pete frowned. It didn't seem as though Chris could see what was so obvious to Pete— that scenes like this weren't doing him one bit of good. The minister who had offered them the use of his church basement for tonight had almost withdrawn the offer when he saw how easygoing Chris was with the girl, not to mention how he'd offended the people standing around.

If Chris himself couldn't see how he was damaging his own reputation, others certainly could. Jude, for sure. Jude was an obnoxious jerk, but Pete couldn't help agreeing with the guy sometimes.

"I feel like tearing my hair out!" Jude had confided to Pete that evening. "How's he ever going to get anywhere? He's the hottest property in the country, but he has no idea how to market himself. The guy needs management, definitely."

"I'm not sure he really sees it that way."

"So?" Jude shrugged. "However he sees his—his mission, or whatever, he still needs to market it. And I'm starting to worry. Remember how things used to be when we started out?"

"Oh yeah. Boy, everybody loved Chris Davidson then, didn't they?" Pete felt almost nostalgic. "But the stuff he was doing then—the big miracles, feeding the crowds, you know? He was giving them just what they wanted."

"Exactly! So why does he have to go around alienating people now? You know, he's been talking about going off in the woods somewhere, away from it all. Somebody offered him the use of this hunting and fishing lodge up north, and Chris was nodding and smiling like it was a good idea to go off to the woods and live like a hermit! How is that going to help his PR?"

Pete didn't like all of Jude's talk about PR and management, but he worried about Chris and how many people seemed to be lining up against him. Thoughts tumbled through his mind, making sleep impossible. He got up, trying not to disturb his wife and kids, and picked his way carefully across the room through a tangle of sleeping bodies.

Pete pushed open the door marked "Exit" and crept upstairs. It was colder up here. He stood in the cramped foyer, shivering, until he noticed a sliver of light under the sanctuary door.

He pulled open the door that led into the sanctuary. One dim light burned there, up near the pulpit. A man sat on the front pew, leaning forward, looking up at the stained-glass window above the choir loft. Pete could hear Chris's voice, though he couldn't pick out the words.

Chris's voice rose a little, and though Pete still couldn't pick out all the words, he could clearly hear the anguish, the pleading, in his tone. Disconnected phrases drifted back. "How can I . . . ?" "Why don't they . . . ?" "I try so hard . . ."

Chris's voice broke off, his head dropped. He sat in silence, holding his head in his hands. After what seemed a very long time, Pete heard him begin to speak again, his voice calm and steady this time. His face was once again raised to the towering stained-glass window. Involuntarily, Pete moved forward, straining to hear. Again, he caught only phrases. "Thank You, Father . . ."; ". . . know You're with me . . ."; ". . . Your strength . . ."

Pete stepped back, out of the sanctuary and into darkness again. He didn't understand all that he'd seen, but he was glad he'd waited to hear some kind of conclusion. The picture of Chris Davidson in pain and discouragement was more than his heart could carry.

The next day, Chris showed no signs of the past night's wakefulness. They went to the biggest shopping mall in the area, and Chris started to speak in the parking lot just outside the main entrance. Before long, the crowds had grown huge. Shoppers who crowded the mall to enjoy holiday bargains stood shoulder-to-shoulder in the frost-tinged air, listening to the ringing voice that had no trouble carrying to the back of the crowd. As always, the children squeezed closest to Chris.

"This world is a dark place," Chris was saying. "Much of the time we seem to be surrounded by darkness, groping to find our way. But it doesn't have to be dark in this world. I've come to bring light into this world. I am this world's Light, and if you follow me, you'll never have to live in darkness again!"

A voice close to Chris broke the silence. "So we're supposed to believe you're sent from God, just because you say so yourself?" Other voices joined in. "Haven't got much backup for that claim, have you?" one challenged.

Pete, walking towards the mall entrance, didn't hear the specific words of reply. He could pretty much predict what Chris would say—scenes like this were getting pretty common. Once he was inside, the whole scene in the courtyard had an air of unreality to it. He turned and walked aimlessly down the mall.

The huge bank of TV screens in an electronics store caught his eye. One or two were showing a soap opera, but almost all displayed the same program, a talk show. Pete was about to turn away when he realized that the panel was discussing Chris. He stood transfixed as a blond woman, her face reproduced several times in various sizes and degrees of hi-definition, earnestly told the host that Mr. Davidson was doing a lot of good.

"I couldn't disagree more," another panelist interrupted, leaning forward. He was a gray-haired man in a three-piece suit; Pete vaguely recognized him as an important local politician, but couldn't place his name till it flashed across the bottom of the screen. "By appearing to do good, Chris Davidson is actually doing tremendous harm. This man genuinely wants us to believe he is God! Simple, ignorant, easily led people will listen to him and believe that he really does hold the cure to their own problems and to society's problems." He looked at his fellow panelists, then straight back into the camera. "This is no trivial matter. Chris Davidson must be stopped."

Chapter Nine

As Martha filled the sink to wash dishes, the doorbell cut across the sound of running water. Drying her hands on her apron, Martha hurried down the two flights of stairs between the Castillo apartment and the front porch.

When she opened the door, she didn't recognize the dark-haired woman who stood uncertainly on the porch until the stranger half-smiled and said, "Martha . . . ?"

It seemed too impossible, too absurd. "Maria?" Martha stepped aside and swung the door wider. "Come in . . . Maria. Yes, of course. I only thought . . . you've changed."

"Well, ten years." Maria shrugged, moving into the hall. She carried a small, cheap-looking tote bag and a large purse. "I guess I have changed. You have, too, a little bit."

Martha put her hand up to her own hair. Maria had the same dark hair and eyes and fine features. But her beauty looked cheapened, tired, used up. Her face lacked the sparkling vivacity that had marked her as a teenager.

Inside the apartment, Martha reached out to take her sister's coat. She examined it quickly as she hung it up; like the tote bag, it was tawdry. Wherever Maria had spent the past ten years, it hadn't been a big step up from Lancer Avenue.

In the kitchen, the two women sat down. Both perched on the edge of their chairs. Maria's eyes flicked around the room, resting for the briefest moment on her old school picture. "Well—this place hasn't changed much," she said at last.

"No . . . well, the fridge is new."

"Oh, really?" Maria asked politely.

"Yes, the old one finally gave out," Martha said, glad to have found something to talk about. Maria seemed to be keeping back a smile. "I could get by with it, but it wasn't so good. I finally got this one after Larry moved back home."

"Larry's home?" Maria asked. "But I thought . . ." She let the question trail off.

"Oh, they broke up. Sally left him when the baby was only about two. He's been living here ever since."

"And . . . Mom?"

"She died about a year after Larry came home," Martha said quickly. She stood up and went over to the sink. "Lung cancer."

"Oh, I'm so sorry," said Maria, so low the words could hardly be heard.

Martha looked at her sister out of the corner of her eye. Maria was simply dressed, in jeans and a hoodie. She was smiling again. She seemed contented, at peace in a way she hadn't been when she was younger.

After a moment, Maria picked up a dishtowel and began to dry the dishes as Martha washed. "I don't suppose you've heard anything about—Simon, have you?" Maria asked, hesitating the barest second before the name.

"It's hard not to hear of him," Martha replied. "He's a real big shot now, owns a bunch of businesses—they say he's running for mayor. Hasn't been in the news so much lately though, I hear he's been sick."

Maria didn't comment. Martha was nervous. Mentioning

Simon brought them dangerously close to the memory of the last time Maria had stood in this kitchen.

"I think I owe it to you to tell you," Maria said after a moment, "that I haven't lived a very . . . nice life since I left here."

"Oh?"

"I'm sure you don't want to know all the details. But I thought I should tell you because—because you may not want me home, knowing what I've done."

Martha slowly rubbed a scouring pad along the bottom of a frying pan, scraping away the burned-on bits. "I'm sure I wouldn't approve of whatever you've done, Maria," she said, "but I turned you out of this house once. I won't do it again."

"As long as you're sure," Maria said.

Martha shrugged. "Anyway, your brother wouldn't let me. Do you know how happy he'll be to see you again?"

Maria's face was alight. "Oh, I hope so! I want to see him again too. When will he be home?"

"He gets off work at five, so he shouldn't be much longer."

"There's one thing I do have to tell you," Maria continued. "I need to explain why I came back, after all this."

"Yes—I was wondering."

"Don't worry—I haven't come home to freeload. I'm going to get a job, maybe as a waitress or something. I'll even get my own place, if it doesn't work out with me staying here. But I had to see you again, to come home. I wish Mom was still alive—I needed to tell all of you I was sorry for what I did to you, and . . . and forgive you for what you did to me."

"Isn't it a bit late for that?"

"No. I couldn't have come back any sooner. I never would have come back at all but—I've changed. I met someone . . ."

Martha, looking down at the sink, raised her eyebrows. Maria laughed.

"Not like that—not a man. I mean, not just a man. His name is Chris Davidson, and he—"

"You know Chris Davidson?"

"Yes, do you know who he is?"

"He's eaten at this table more times than I can count . . . I worked with him here in Marselles when he first started preaching . . ."

Maria whirled to face Martha, clasping both her hands. Her face glowed with an excitement greater even than the excitement she'd shown at the thought of seeing her brother.

"Martha, you know him! And Larry too? How wonderful! I was so afraid of explaining to you, so afraid you wouldn't understand what he did for me—but if you know him, then you already understand. Oh, this is so much better than I expected!"

"Well, I don't know him as well as some of the others do—" Martha demurred, drawing her hands away from Maria's. It was, she now realized, the absolute truth. She had cooked and cleaned for Chris and his friends. They had slept on her living room floor, and she had washed and mended their clothes. She had worked as hard for Chris as had any of his followers in Marselles—Erica or Bob Washington or Audrey Johnson—or any of them. She and Larry had even gone along on one of his trips back last summer. But she didn't know him as many of the others did—as her own brother did, as her sister now seemed to.

Maria wasn't put off. "Oh, but you're so lucky! To have spent so much time with him—I'd love to see him again. I need to—there's so much I still have to learn."

"How did you meet him?"

Maria didn't answer for a moment. "It was sort of an awkward situation. I was in trouble, being accused of something, and I suppose you could say he stuck up for me. But that wasn't all. He told me I was forgiven—you know how he says he can forgive sins? That sounds so crazy, but you know, as soon as he says it, you know it's true. Once he's told you you're forgiven, you don't wonder anymore about this business of him saying he's God because, you know, only God could forgive you that way. But I suppose you know all that, since you've known him so long."

"Yes . . . well." She did know, because Larry and the others talked like that, too, about sins being forgiven. Hers? She had shied away from conversation with Chris Davidson partly out of the fear that he might offer to forgive her sins. And the only reply that came to her mind was ludicrous—*I have no sins.* Of course, you couldn't say that; everyone had sins, but Martha's problems had nothing to do with whatever sins she might have committed. Most of her misfortunes were the fault of other people, or of circumstances, not of her own doing. She knew that something must be wrong with this reasoning, but all she could clearly figure out was that Maria had had her sins—probably really awful ones—forgiven, and now Chris, like all the others, would love Maria best.

But the fact remained; she could not turn her sister away again. Especially if she was a friend of Chris Davidson's. Martha turned back to her dishwashing. "I'm glad you've come home, Maria." It was not quite the truth, but it was as close as she was likely to get for now.

Chapter Ten

"You might as well not even be in the kitchen if you can't work any faster than that. Why don't you go out and hang around the men, like usual?" Martha was more annoyed at herself than at her sister when she heard the words leave her mouth, but she couldn't call them back. Frozen in the act of peeling a potato, Maria stared back at her with wide uncertain eyes.

"Hey, I resent that sexist remark," Andy Johnson said in mock indignation. "Some of 'the men' are on kitchen duty, too, don't forget."

"And where would we be without you?" Mary Davidson patted Andy lightly on the back as she crossed the kitchen. Pulling up a stool opposite Maria, she added, "We really do need two people at this. I'm finished with the salads; I'll give you a hand." She picked up a potato and an extra peeler and set to work.

Martha turned back to the counter where she was working on a roast. Once again, everyone had been sweet and kind and helpful and had made her look just awful. They were all so careful about Maria's feelings. But what about hers?

For more than a month now, Chris Davidson and many of his friends and followers had been staying at this isolated hunting lodge. Martha, Maria, and Larry had driven up just two weeks ago, and Martha had quickly found her niche helping out in the kitchen along with Chris's mother, Mary, and a few others. Though the lodge was supposed to be a safe place away from the storm of controversy Chris aroused in bigger centers, it in fact acted like a magnet, drawing people from all over who wanted to talk to Chris and learn more about him. Martha sometimes found herself organizing dinner for as many as sixty people.

Being on her feet all through supper didn't improve her mood any. But at least in the kitchen she was spared the endless clamor of voices. Her brother and sister were among the group gathered out in the main room. Martha still remembered with a sharp sting an occasion at her own apartment back in Marselles, when she'd tried to get Maria to come help her in the kitchen and Chris had told her that she, Martha, would be better off being out talking with him than slaving over the meal. She'd been so hurt and angry. But the truth was, it was almost a relief when everyone else was out with Chris, and Martha could have the kitchen to herself. With supper over and cleared away, she shooed out the rest of the helpers so she could finish cleaning up on her own.

By the time she got the plates and glasses loaded into the dishwasher and began scrubbing the big pots by hand, the group had begun singing out by the fireplace. "Day Is Dying in the West"—Martha hummed along; she'd always liked that song.

The dishes were actually done before she noticed that the singing had ended and only Chris Davidson's voice and the crackling fire broke the silence. She finished wiping the counter by the sink, wrung out a cloth, and stepped over to wipe down the serving counter. From there she could see the fireplace at the far end of the room and saw Chris's face, lit by firelight, as he talked.

He was telling a story Martha had often heard him tell before—the story of the sheep that was lost so the shepherd had to go and find it. Of all his stories, that was the one people liked best and asked to hear again and again.

When the story was finished, a child's voice spoke up from somewhere in the crowded room, "Tell another story!"

"You want another story?" Chris replied, laughing. "All right, here's another one that's a lot like the story about the sheep—but it's different too. It starts out on a ranch, owned by a rich and prosperous cattle farmer. This man had two sons— the older, a steady, reliable, responsible boy; the younger, a bit impulsive and reckless."

Martha had finished wiping the counter, but she stayed leaning there, listening to this new story.

"One day the younger son, tired of the tedious daily chores, went to his father and said, 'Dad, this life isn't for me. I need to go to the city, see new places, and meet new people—broaden my horizons.'

"His father said, 'But how do you plan to support yourself in the city?'

" 'Um, well,' the son replied, 'that's kind of what I wanted to talk to you about. Do you think you could give me my share of the inheritance now—what I'm supposed to get when you die?' "

The listeners sat attentively as Chris continued the story by relating the son's escapades in the city. His marvelous storyteller's voice dropped as the boy's fortunes fell, and he spoke sadly of the loss of his money and friends, and how he was forced at last to work as a janitor in a run-down, rat-infested tenement building. His eyes rested first on one, then on another, of the group.

Martha could see Maria's face turned eagerly up to Chris's. Did his eyes rest a little longer on hers as he described that lonely boy's sufferings? Yes, Martha thought, and then his gaze went tenderly to others in the group who she knew had left behind terribly mixed-up lives to follow him. Each of them, no doubt, identified with that poor lost boy. She found her own thoughts turning to the forgotten older brother, diligently working at home, probably getting little thanks for it.

But all was going well in the story now; the younger son had come to his senses and was returning home. "He had a little speech all prepared," Chris said. "He was going to tell his father, 'Dad, I've done wrong in your eyes and in the eyes of God. I don't deserve to be your son anymore. Can you take me on as a hired hand?' But he never got through the speech. His father saw him coming when he was still a long way down the road, and ran to him, enfolded him in his arms, and cried on his shoulder.

"The father told everyone in the house to prepare a big celebration dinner for that night. But in the midst of the preparations, his older son came to him and said, 'What's all this? All these years I've stayed home and obeyed your orders and slaved away like a servant, and you've never bought me a new suit or thrown a party for me. Then this irresponsible jerk shows up, after wasting all your money on booze and prostitutes, no doubt, and you act like it's the end of the world!'

"But his father said, 'Son, you are always here with me, and everything I have is yours. But we must celebrate, because your brother was dead and is alive again; he was lost and has been found.' "

Chris Davidson's eyes swept over the crowd and up to meet Martha's. She stood frozen as he held her with his gaze. She twisted the washcloth in her hands, then abruptly turned away, and pulled down the screen between her kitchen and the rest of the lodge.

She moved across the dimly lit kitchen and sat down at the table. Her hands continued to play with the damp dishcloth as her mind raced. So Chris had seen, and known, how she felt all along. Two brothers, of course, not two sisters—how clever of him to disguise the story. Her throat constricted; her fingers clenched the dishrag.

She didn't hear anyone come in. Nonetheless, she wasn't startled when she felt hands touch her shoulders. Of course, he would be there.

Saying nothing, he sat down across the table from her. He took the twisted cloth from her hands and laid those hands flat on the table. Then he covered them with his own hands, bigger and even more calloused and work-worn than her own. She could feel his gaze steady on her, till finally she was forced to lift her own eyes to meet his. The silence lasted a long time.

"It was a good story," Martha said at last.

Chris shrugged. "Like any story, everyone will get something different out of it. What did you get from my story, Martha Castillo?"

"You never finished it."

"I suppose I didn't. But most of them"—he nodded toward the outer room—"don't need to hear the rest. Most of them are encouraged to know that God accepts the sinner back after he's wandered away. Only a few people need to be reminded that you don't have to wander far to cut yourself off from the Father's love."

"So . . . how does the story end?" Martha's heart still pounded, but in the intensity of the moment she was forgetting her fear, growing bolder.

"That depends," he replied, "on what the older son says to the Father."

Martha glanced around the kitchen, focusing on irrelevant

objects—a spoon, a bowl, a calendar. She swallowed. "What if—if the older . . . sister . . . says to the Father, 'I'm sorry I've been so selfish. I was jealous of the love You gave my sister because I never realized all the love You had for me, all along. I've acted like a servant who expects to be paid, instead of like Your child who knows she's loved.' "

She was looking straight at him now, and although his face stayed perfectly solemn, his eyes shone. "Then the Father will say, 'My daughter, don't you see that you could never earn My love by your good deeds, any more than your sister could lose My love by doing wrong? For both of you the answer is the same—My love is there; you only have to accept it.' "

Finally, then, her tears broke loose, running hot down her flushed cheeks. She did not reach up to wipe them away, because Chris Davidson was still holding her hands.

Chapter Eleven

The telephone in the lodge shrilled across the early morning sounds. Pete picked it up. The line crackled with static.

"Hello—Peter, is that you?"

"Yes," he said uncertainly, trying to place the voice.

"Is Chris there? I haven't been able to get him on his cell or anything—" The woman sounded as if she were speaking through tears.

"No, sorry, he's gone out. Cell service is really spotty up here, and—"

"Pete, I have to talk to him, this is really urgent—"

"Is this Maria? I didn't recognize your voice."

"Yes—Pete, when Chris comes in, please, please tell him we need him here right away. It's Larry—he's very, very sick. We need Chris here—"

"What is it, Maria? What's wrong with him?"

The note of alarm in Pete's voice had caught the attention of the half-dozen or so people in the room, and they were quiet, trying to gather the bad news.

"Meningitis. There've been several cases here in Marselles. Larry is . . ." Her voice broke. A muffled moment later, Martha came on the line. She, too, though more controlled, sounded shaken.

"The doctors say his chances may not be very good, Peter. Larry has been asking for Chris."

"Of course, Martha. I'm sure Chris will be there as soon as he can."

When Pete hung up and told the news to the others, they all agreed with him. Might as well start loading up the van, because Chris would want to be on the road right away. With public opinion against Chris Davidson running so high right now, Marselles, so close to the city, was a dangerous place for him to be. But when had danger ever kept him away from someone who needed him?

It was only a month or so since the Castillos had left the lodge to return to Marselles, after spending nearly the whole winter with Chris. Pete liked Larry Castillo—he was an easygoing, down-to-earth guy who fit in well with the crowd and got along with everyone. It was impossible to imagine him lying in a hospital bed, watched by worried doctors.

With tension crackling in the air all day, it seemed almost unbearable that Chris and the others were late getting back. Pete tried several times during the day to reach Chris, John, or Matt on their phones but couldn't get through. It was already dark when they pulled up. As soon as Chris stepped into the lodge, a clamor of voices tried to tell him the news.

Pete's only worry was that the sisters' message had taken so long to reach Chris. Now that he knew, there was really no need to fear. He understood the relief that had flooded Martha's trembling voice at the assurance that Chris would come. How often had he himself thought that if Audrey or one of the kids were sick, he'd feel completely relaxed knowing Chris Davidson, who'd healed so many people, was right there! But Chris didn't even need to be "right there" to work a miracle. They'd all seen him the day he told that businessman his son was cured—and hadn't the man later received a call saying his son's condition had begun to improve at just the time Chris had spoken? No, as long as he knew about Larry, there was no cause for anxiety.

Chris's words echoed Peter's thoughts. "There's no need to be afraid. Larry's going to live." Then, as murmurs of relief swept the room, he added, "This is happening for a reason. Larry's illness will bring honor to God and reveal God's Son to the world." For a moment, a look of pain, almost of regret, flickered across his face.

Pete expected that the next thing they heard from the Castillos would be that Larry's condition had improved—if not that he'd made a miraculous recovery. Instead, the morning's news was worse. Throughout the following day, Maria and Martha sent e-mails and text messages updating their friends on the situation and asking, over and over, if Chris could please come to see Larry now, before it was too late.

"Chris has been acting funny since he heard the news," Jim Fisher observed on Saturday morning—almost two full days, now, since they'd heard the news. There had been no news so far from Marselles, and neither Martha nor Maria was picking up her phone. "All yesterday he was really tense, almost like he wanted to go, but he was being kept here against his will. You know what I mean?"

Pete arched a stone overhead and watched it splash into the water. "You mark my words," he said. "There's something fishy going on here."

Sunday afternoon. The miles of road unrolled beneath the heavily loaded blue van. Chris had announced at lunchtime that he was going to see Larry Castillo, and everyone at the lodge seemed to have come along, a caravan of cars following the blue van to Marselles.

Even now, though, they weren't taking the most direct route to Marselles. They were puttering along winding back roads.

"I thought we might stop soon for the night," Chris said, into the silence.

"Uh, boss—" Pete said, "we could make Marselles tonight if we press on. Don't you want to see Larry?"

Chris checked the rearview mirror. "Larry is asleep by now," he said with the calm certainty he always used in telling them things he couldn't possibly know. "I'll wake him up when I get there."

"Oh—did you finally hear something from Maria? I suppose if he's getting a good night's sleep that means he's getting better," Andy put in.

Chris didn't answer for a moment. Something like a sigh escaped his lips, very quietly. "I didn't mean that kind of sleep," he said at last. "Larry's dead."

The relief Pete felt at being on the road melted, revealing dark patches of fear underneath.

When they finally got into Marselles, Chris took the exit nearest the Lancer Avenue Community Center. The building looked quiet, with only a few cars around, but inside they found Martha Castillo sitting in the empty office, her arms folded tight as if trying to hold herself together. She looked up and met Chris's eyes as the men entered the building.

She came forward to meet him, her voice rough-edged from spent tears. He took both her hands. "Why didn't you come? If only you'd been here, I know he wouldn't have died. But even now—" she swallowed and went on, "I still believe God will give you whatever you ask for. That's why I don't understand—" The walls were down again; she clung to him as if he were life itself, though Pete guessed she'd been angry only moments before.

"Your brother will live again, Martha—"

She turned away, and pulled her hands back from his grasp. "I know," she said wearily. "I believe in the resurrection at the end of the world, and I believe Larry will be raised then . . ."

The sound of Chris's voice seemed to pull her toward him. "I am resurrection and life. Anyone who believes in me still has life, even in death. And death can never really touch someone who is with me. Do you believe this?"

Martha's voice was simple and steady. "Yes, I believe that you are God's chosen One, the One sent to us."

It's true, Pete realized. *He is life.* You couldn't imagine death in his presence. He recalled those two strange incidents—the sick little girl who had died before they got to the house; the young man whose grieving mother they had visited at his deathbed. In both cases, cynics had tried to explain away what seemed impossible, which was easy to do as few people besides Chris Davidson's close friends had been there, but Pete knew he'd seen Chris defeat death. Now his words fanned hope wildly alive again.

Maria arrived just then, sobbing. She'd never had Martha's need to control her emotions, to hold herself back. She broke away from the people around her and ran to Chris, clinging to his arms. Above their heads, Chris's head, too, was bowed. "Have you had the funeral yet?" he asked in an odd voice.

"Yesterday afternoon," said Erica Washington. "I thought we should wait, but Martha insisted she didn't want a viewing or any big service."

"Can you take me there?" Chris asked.

By the time they reached the shabby little cemetery where residents of the Lancer Avenue neighborhood were buried, quite a crowd had gathered. Apart from the people who'd come with them from the lodge, Pete recognized the Castillos' friends from the neighborhood and many of Chris's followers from Marselles, who must have been waiting for him to arrive. Other faces were unfamiliar, and looked curious rather than sympathetic.

Larry's grave was easy to spot; the mound of fresh earth stood out among the grass-covered plots that surrounded it. For a moment, no one said anything as Chris stood at the foot of the grave, his head bowed. Then he looked up at the people around him.

"Dig it up," he commanded.

There was no response except a shocked murmur from the crowd. "He's been dead since Friday . . ." Martha protested weakly.

"Didn't I tell you that if you believed in God, you would see His glory?" Chris challenged. It was the voice no one dared resist.

"There's shovels over there by the caretaker's building," he heard someone call. People were moving now—some pushing closer to the grave, others moving farther back. Someone put a shovel in Pete's hand. But he handed it to Matt before the job was done and stepped back to stand beside Audrey.

Holding Audrey close, Pete noticed that many of the bystanders had their phones out to snap pictures and video. *Whatever happens here, it'll be all over the Internet in an hour,* he realized. He resisted the urge to slap the phone out of the hand of a man standing nearby. *Maybe it's best this way,* he told himself. Whatever Chris did, there would be plenty of witnesses, and no shortage of evidence.

There was a commotion near the grave itself now, as more people pushed forward to see and record the moment. He heard the metallic scrape of latches being turned, heard a woman's voice scream, "No, don't—!" and then a chorus of gasps and shouts.

Craning to see over and between people's heads, Pete saw

Andy and John standing in the grave itself, bending down to open the coffin, and then saw them pull Larry Castillo to his feet. Briefly, through the jostle of people in front of him, Pete glimpsed the perfectly healthy, pleasantly bewildered face of the man who had helped him fix the dishwasher at the lodge. Larry was wearing a suit, but otherwise, he looked just like himself. Maria and Martha were hugging him, people crowded close, trying to touch him and take pictures with him.

Pete found himself jostled to the rear of the crowd. A man in front of him turned around and he saw that it was Chris.

He still looked tired, but no longer tense. "You were right," Pete said. "He's alive. And people did see God's glory." He laid a hand on Chris's arm. "So—it was worth all the pain, wasn't it?"

Chris smiled. "Yes. But it's not over. This is just the beginning."

Chapter Twelve

"Something's up, and I don't like it." Jim Fisher paced around the dingy hotel room. He paused by the window and looked nervously down at the news van parked in the street below.

"Relax, Jim. Of course something's up. Something's been up ever since we left the lodge. You're not supposed to like it."

Leaving his disgruntled friend fuming in front of the window, Pete strolled out into the hall and knocked on the door of the room adjacent to the one he had just left. He sat down on the floor next to Nat and picked up the copy of this week's *Time* magazine, which Nat had just tossed aside. Not that he hadn't seen it before. It had hit the newsstands yesterday and since then practically every one of Chris's companions had memorized the lead story.

The cover showed the now-famous picture of Chris Davidson and Larry Castillo at the cemetery, gripping each other's hands tightly. Across the picture, yellow letters blazed: "CHRIS DAVIDSON: FRAUD, FANATIC, OR FAITH HEALER?"

Pete leafed through the article before tossing it aside, probably for the same reason Nat had—because he ran across a ghastly, unflattering shot of himself, Nat, and Andy. At least they'd balanced it with a shot of Simon and Thad together, hinting at the peace and harmony that reigned among Chris's followers. Sometimes.

Two short raps sounded before the door burst open. Chris stood there, his face alight with excitement. The preoccupied air that had weighed him down since their return to Marselles was gone.

"Come on!" he called to them, laughing at their startled expressions. "Did you think I'd left you? Did you think you were going to sit here and brood forever? Not a chance! The time has come! Let's get going!"

They were all on their feet. "What do you want us to do, boss?" Pete asked.

Chris met Pete's eyes with a grin. He handed him a slip of paper with a few words written on it. "Go look up this address. The man there has a car I need to borrow. Tell him I need it." Noticing Tomas's dubious glance, he assured them, "He'll understand."

"I wonder what he meant?" John mused as they drove to the address. "About this being the time?"

"Well, you know how many times someone's tried to get him to make some kind of political move, and he always says 'My time hasn't come yet'?" Pete glanced at the others for affirmation. "Well, now I guess it's time. He's making his move."

"I think you're right," John agreed. "But I've got a feeling that whatever kind of move he's going to make, it's not going to be what people are expecting."

"Whatever it is, I'd like to know what borrowing a car has to do with it," said Tomas.

The car turned out to be a vintage convertible. As Chris had assured them, the owner was quite willing to lend it, although he seemed to have no more idea what it would be used for than they did. The top was down, and Pete drove it back to the hotel in style, thrilled to be driving such a well-maintained beauty of a vehicle.

Back at the hotel, the lobby was crowded with familiar faces. The night before, Chris had invited only his twelve closest followers to go to the city with him. But this morning, the Castillos were there, and Audrey, and the Washingtons—in fact, most of Chris Davidson's supporters from back in Marselles, and from other nearby towns as well.

Within fifteen minutes, Pete found himself behind the wheel of the open car again, this time with Chris in the passenger's seat and Jim and John Fisher in the backseat. Behind them, the blue van and a long line of dusty cars and trucks stretched out like a working-class motorcade.

"Head up to Grandview, Pete," Chris instructed him, "and take it nice and slow." He was wearing a shirt and slacks Pete hadn't seen on him before—still casual, but dressier than the familiar jeans and T-shirt. He was clearly prepared for some kind of an event.

Grandview Avenue was crowded with shoppers. Pete forced himself to drive slowly, but it was hardly necessary. Within minutes, the unusual procession had attracted attention, and people were clustering on the sidewalks to see the man whose face had become so familiar. He could hear the shouts of "It's him! Chris Davidson!" and out of the corner of his eye, he saw people waving and holding up their phones for pictures. Chris smiled and waved to the crowd as regally as any world leader on a state visit.

As they reached the intersection of Grandview and Wellington, Pete saw that crowds of people had lined up on Wellington east of Grandview. "They're expecting us to turn down there!" John yelled, leaning forward from the backseat.

"Well, do we?" Pete turned to Chris.

"Sure!"

Pete turned right onto Wellington.

There was no other traffic, though double-parked vehicles on both sides narrowed the street. People sat in cars or on top of them, or stood along the street, cheering as the white convertible inched its way along. Driving so slowly, Pete was free to look more closely at Chris. Instead of smiling and waving into a faceless crowd, as most leaders would, Chris Davidson seemed to seek out individual faces and smile at them. It was the same as it had always been—for him, there were no crowds, only individuals.

Perhaps that warm personal glance was what caused people to begin rushing forward into the street. First one, then another, then a flood of them rushed the car, reaching in to touch Chris. Teenagers leaned over the side of the open car trying to snap smartphone pictures of themselves with Chris before he drove on. He clasped hands with as many as he could, and the crowds in front of the car parted to let them move on.

They cruised past the town hall and turned left up the hill toward the city park. Again, the crowd seemed to have anticipated their route, for the spring sunlight glinted off the hoods of innumerable cars in the parking lot. As Pete slowed the convertible to a stop just inside the park's entrance gates, throngs of people surged around the car.

Of course, the police had shown up by now. Three or four officers vainly struggled to keep the yelling crowd under control, while another pushed his way through to the convertible.

"Mr. Davidson, sir, this is disturbing the peace, you know. Can't you keep your people under control? Calm them down!"

Chris just shook his head at the officer, half-laughing. "I can't do it, officer. Not now. If I were to make these people be quiet, then the rocks themselves would start shouting. It's time to celebrate!"

The officer retreated, swallowed by the crowd. Chris climbed out of the car. Pete wasn't sure what he—or the crowd—expected. Perhaps for Chris to stand up in the car and start talking to them, as he had been known to do before. Instead, he moved among the people, touching, talking, and healing the sick who were thrust toward him. For a while, Pete lost sight of Chris or any of his friends as strangers milled around. Quite a while passed before people began asking where Chris was and discovering that no one knew. John sidled up to Pete and asked, "Have you seen him lately?"

"No, not since he got out of the car. He does have this way of disappearing in crowds," Pete muttered.

"Come with me. I've got a hunch . . ." John grabbed Pete's elbow and led him through the crowd.

Beyond the throng clustered around the cars, people sat in small groups on the grass and on picnic tables. The place had a holiday atmosphere—and something that went beyond the regular holiday season, a mood of expectation, of hope and change.

They found Chris well apart from the crowd, in a quiet clearing on the hill that overlooked the city. He was standing quietly, and as they drew near they saw that he was crying. It shocked Pete, as it had on the day Larry Castillo came back from the dead. Looking out at the city, he repeated, "If only . . . if only . . . I wanted to take care of you all, to gather you together like a mother gathers her children—but you rejected me. I wanted to protect you . . . but now it's too late."

Unable to stop himself, Pete sprang forward and grabbed Chris's arm. "No, boss! You can't say that!"

He turned to look at Pete, an unreadable expression in his now-clear brown eyes. John said, "Pete—" in a warning tone, but Pete hurried on. "I mean, how can you say they've rejected you? Look at the response you got out there! This isn't the end, this is just the beginning!"

"Yes, Pete, it is the beginning. But it's not the beginning they're expecting."

Chapter Thirteen

The day was warm. Maria considered slipping off her jacket, but, thinking of the people standing around, decided she didn't want to. Instead, she pulled it closer, though the spring sunshine poured down on her shoulders as she followed Chris and the others into the Randall Hotel and Convention Center.

During this holiday week, the city was host for a nationwide conference on "Religion and Society." Every major religious group was represented, as well as several minor ones. Along with seminars and workshops, there were public events—concerts, panel discussions, worship services—planned throughout the week, culminating in a huge ecumenical worship service at the end of the week.

"You've got to admit, his timing is perfect," John Fisher commented as they strolled through the Convention Center lobby. "He brings your brother back to life and captures everyone's attention, and then, just at the time of year when everyone's likely to be thinking about religion anyway, he makes this big mysterious drive through the city and disappears again. Now this conference tops it all off."

Maria surveyed the display in front of them. The banner

draped across it proclaimed the name of a popular TV evange-
list. Women with hairspray-stiff curls offered "free" prayer medallions in return for donations. A few booths down, a slightly
larger crowd milled around a man dressed in flowing robes who
was demonstrating meditation exercises. At the next table, people were browsing CDs and DVDs by a well-known religious
singer, while across the lobby a group of earnest biblical scholars
selling hardcover books had collected no crowd at all.

"From the sublime to the ridiculous," John remarked, rais-
ing an eyebrow.

"I don't see a whole lot of sublime around here," Maria
replied.

Then they heard the crash.

It could have been the sound of a door crashing open, except
that the hotel had only revolving doors. Actually, it was the large
notice board welcoming visitors to the conference, which stood
at the front of the huge lobby. When everyone else in the room
turned around, Maria turned too, with a sinking feeling that she
knew what she'd see.

Chris Davidson stood there, one man alone in a crowded
room, not unusually large or tall, completely commanding
the attention of everyone there. The toppled notice board lay
sprawled at Chris's feet, and in his right hand he carried some
kind of stick.

A corridor had suddenly opened through the middle of the
lobby, and down this Chris Davidson strode. His ringing voice
silenced the murmurs and echoed to every corner.

"Get this foolishness out of here!" he commanded. He barely
glanced at a display of books topped by a large blow-up picture
of the author; he simply reached out and pushed it over. "You
have taken the vital truth God has given you, His Word and His
message and His mission, and turned it into a money-making

machine!" Reaching the table with the prayer medallions, he flipped it over with his left hand, spilling the tawdry merchandise on the floor.

The hairsprayed proprietors of the booth stumbled over spectators in their eagerness to back away from Chris. He cut a wide swath through the room, taking in the books, pamphlets, and religious paraphernalia with unconcealed disgust. The now familiar clicking of dozens of phone cameras punctuated the babble of people backing away from Chris Davidson. When his voice rose again, the murmur of the crowd ceased instantly.

"You think you can put God into boxes, into books, into seminar rooms! You think you can analyze and dissect and explain 'religion and society'? What would you do with a religion that turned your society completely upside down?"

He stood still in the center of the room, a powerful and vaguely menacing figure. He said nothing more, but turned and walked to the far side of the lobby. People murmured, stirred, and shifted position. At the edge of the lobby clustered a group of people in wheelchairs, probably waiting for the faith healer who was supposed to speak at 10:00. It was toward these people that Chris walked, and they were the first to call his name and reach out to him.

Half an hour later, the people wearing the official red-and-white convention badges had not returned, but more and more people thronged into the lobby of the Randall Hotel to see Chris Davidson. He healed sick people, talked to them, and told stories. He perched on top of a bench at the far end of the lobby, and the people sat, knelt, and stood ten deep around him.

"I absolutely cannot believe this," Maria said to Audrey Johnson, shaking her head.

"I know, isn't it incredible?" The two women watched as a small group of men in pinstriped suits approached Chris. Maria wondered if this would mean trouble, but whatever they said to him, Chris must have had a good answer. After a short conversation, the men in suits edged away, talking among themselves. One went over to speak to a uniformed security guard.

"Did you see cops outside? I'm never sure whether to trust the police or not," Maria said to Audrey, when a stranger standing nearby interrupted.

"I figure the police are waiting for their moment," he said. "Your man must know that there's an awful lot of people who'd like him out of the way."

"But he's here, every day at the hotel," Maria said. "If they want to find him—"

"Sure, but they're not going to take him here in front of everyone, are they? Can you see the publicity?"

"But what can they arrest him for anyway? Disturbing the peace, maybe, that'd be about it."

The man snorted. "Doesn't matter. Nobody wants to see Chris Davidson go to trial and get a fine or a short jail sentence. They've been digging around for months, trying to find some dirt that could land him in a real scandal like all those other preacher-types. But they can't get anything solid."

"Shouldn't that tell you something?" asked Maria.

The stranger shrugged. "I don't know about that. I don't take sides. I'm not a religious man anyway. I just know that if he's arrested, some kind of 'accident' could happen while he's being held in jail. Or they'll release him into the hands of the right people . . . and make sure justice never gets done."

The world swayed around Maria. "It's impossible," she breathed. "They can't . . ."

Audrey reached out to put a steadying arm around her shoulders. "Don't worry, nothing like that's going to happen. Look at all these people . . . would they let anyone hurt Chris

Davidson? Would *we* let anyone hurt him?"

Maria shook her head, but the words did not untie the knot of fear inside her.

Audrey spoke softly. "Nothing will happen to Chris that he doesn't want to happen. You know that."

Those words, of all words, should have reassured her. But as she looked across the crowded room at Chris, for some reason, Maria's fears remained.

Chapter Fourteen

Candles flickered on the table in honor of the occasion. The holiday dinner, the meal they should all be eating at home with their families. Only, "home" and "family" meant something more than what they used to mean.

The past week had been weird, to put it mildly. Pete found it hard to believe that the drive through the city had taken place only Sunday. Monday had begun with that bizarre scene in the hotel lobby, where Chris had asserted his authority in some way everyone respected, even if they didn't understand.

The rest of the week had been a blur, all centered around the crowds at the hotel who were bent on seeing and hearing Chris Davidson. Every day more people had flocked to him, confirming what Pete kept telling his dubious friends: that people were more supportive of Chris Davidson than ever before.

Yet he couldn't deny that Chris was attracting a lot of negative attention too. That man in the courtyard whose words had so frightened Maria had been the most blunt, but the feeling was not hard to pick up: Chris was putting himself in a dangerous situation.

Chris's words rose out of the murmur of conversation,

jarring harshly with Pete's thoughts. "To tell you the truth," he said, seeming almost matter-of-fact, "I know already that one of you at this table is going to betray me."

Pete didn't know what conversation had led up to that remark, but that statement effectively silenced all further talk. There were a few gasps of "What?" Then, after a moment, Pete saw that Chris's eyes were fixed on his own, and in them he read pain and disappointment so deep that he hardly knew how to respond.

"You can't mean me, boss!" The words were torn out of him.

Chris made no reply, but almost at the same moment, John cried out, "Not me!" Chris looked around the table, meeting each pair of eyes. What each of them wanted, Pete knew, was for Chris to say, "No, of course it's not you. I know you could never do that."

After Chris's strange statement and the shocked denials that followed it, conversation around the candlelit table was reduced almost to whispers. Chris himself broke the silence, gathering everyone's attention with a tone of voice that was oddly ceremonial.

He held in his strong hands the loaf of bread that had lain on the table before him, and he tore off a piece of that loaf and held it up before them.

"Do you see this bread?" Again his eyes moved from one to another. "This bread is my body, which I am giving up for you. Take it and eat it." He handed the loaf of bread to John, seated beside him, who held it as if he were dazed. Finally, John broke off a piece and passed the loaf to Pete.

So the loaf of bread made the circle of the table, each man taking a piece. No one ate until Chris did, and then they all followed his lead. Chewing, Pete thought that it tasted exactly like every other piece of bread he'd ever eaten. But he remembered a sermon Chris Davidson had preached a long time ago, in which he'd compared his body and blood to food and drink, and told people they'd have to eat and drink him to know God's eternal life. Tonight's ritual seemed like a more concrete way of carving that picture into their minds.

Now he lifted a bottle and was pouring the dark liquid into his glass. "This is my blood, which will be spilled as a promise for you." He passed the bottle to John. "Drink this, and remember me."

When everyone had taken a drink, the tension in the room seemed to break, and they were all questioning Chris, wanting to know what his strange words meant. Above the anxious babble of their voices, his broke in. "Don't worry! Don't be afraid! Put your minds at rest. You believe in God, don't you? You believe in me?"

Pete nodded, as the others did.

"Then believe this. My Father has a home—a house with many rooms, and I'm going there to get it ready for you. But I'll be back to get you, to take you all with me." A note of gladness tinged his voice now; they all caught it and held to it. *He's still talking in pictures,* Pete thought, *even now.* The image of the house with many rooms appeared in his mind as a picture of the lodge up north, where they had spent those peaceful, untroubled months.

Chris Davidson went on talking, answering their questions as they ate together. Through it all, Pete heard only one thing: Chris was going to leave them.

Quite abruptly, Chris said, "Come on, it's time to get out of here." Then, as the men shifted in their seats, he added, "First, let's sing a hymn to close our meal."

The song he led them in was one of praise, a favorite of his, and his voice was so strong and clear above the rest that Pete, ever the optimist, dared to hope everything would work out.

No matter what, he knew he would stay by Chris Davidson as long as he could.

He felt it was important, after all that had been said tonight, to let Chris know how he felt. Chris was the last to leave the room, straightening the chairs and table as the others put on their jackets. Pete stopped him at the top of the stairs and laid a hand on his arm.

"Boss—I just want you to know, whatever happens, I'm with you. All the way."

Chris's eyes were terribly tender. "Oh, Rocky," he said softly. The name he'd first called him. Then, "Pete, the enemy wants your soul—he wants to tear you to shreds. But I've prayed for you; prayed God will give you strength to remain faithful."

"What?" Despite the tenderness, the words were a slap in the face after his assurance. "Don't you know I'd follow you anywhere? To prison, to death—anywhere!"

"Would you?" Chris's voice did not accuse, but its edge was sharper. "Peter, before the sun rises tomorrow morning, you'll swear—three times—that you never knew me." He turned away from Pete's shocked glance, from Pete's hand on his arm, and suddenly looking terribly weary, headed down the stairs.

The words haunted Pete all evening, as they followed Chris from the borrowed dining hall to the city park where they sat around in small groups, listening to Chris. Pete found he was drowsy. It had been such a long week, such a roller-coaster of emotions. When he looked at Chris, he saw that Chris didn't look angry, but his eyes held some clear sad knowledge that excluded Pete. So it was a surprise when Chris said to him, "I'm going to walk on a bit farther. Want to come with me?"

"Sure." Pete got to his feet. John darted a quick look at Chris, who nodded to him, and he, too, rose. His brother Jim, next to him, opened drowsy eyes and sat up also.

The three of them followed Chris up the hill, onto the hiking trail between the trees. Pete was vividly reminded of that other time when he, Jim, and John had followed Chris up a hill and seen that strange vision of glory. Like Chris's miracles, that memory gave him a reason to believe during those times when the whole thing seemed ridiculous.

At the top of the hill, the hiking trail leveled off and opened into a small clearing. Here, Chris turned to the three of them. His tired, moonlit face startled Pete. He'd never seen Chris look discouraged or afraid like he did now.

"I need to be alone," Chris said, "but I'd like it if—if you'd wait here for me, and pray with me . . . for me."

He turned away from them and walked to the edge of the clearing, where he knelt on the ground in front of the farthest benches, resting his elbows on the bench and burying his head in his hands.

Chris's voice was audible, barely, and Pete heard the pain, the pleading in his tone. He tried a prayer of his own. "Dear God, I don't understand anything anymore; everything's so messed up . . ." He let his mind drift, sliding in and out of the pictures of memory.

Something nudged the edge of his sleep—a voice or a movement—and he opened his eyes to see James asleep on the bench beside him. Farther away, John lay on the ground, his head cushioned on his arms. And Chris stood a few feet away, wearing that same sad expression and saying something—but Pete slipped quickly back into sleep, and afterward was never sure whether that moonlit tableau was memory or dream. He didn't wake up fully till he heard John shout, "What's that?"

Blinking, Pete turned to look back down the hill. Lights flickered through the trees; voices rose above the sound of car engines and slamming doors.

Pete, James, and John were all on their feet. "Let's see what's going on down there," James said, heading toward the path.

"No, Jim," John said. "Let's wait—"

James was already out of earshot, crashing through the underbrush. Chris walked up behind John and Pete almost silently and placed a hand on each of their shoulders. "It's time," he said simply. His face, though still sad, looked perfectly calm.

Then there were crashing footsteps and bright lights on the path, and suddenly the little clearing was full of men. Pete froze when he saw the one carrying the flashlight: he wore a police uniform.

"Which one is he? Where's Chris Davidson?" The officer held up his flashlight, sweeping its beam across Pete, Chris, and John.

"There he is! That's him!" a chorus of voices called. One man stepped forward from behind the flashlight's glare, and Pete realized with a jolt that there was another familiar face in this crowd. Jude, the college boy, looking a little disheveled and uneasy, walked over to Chris. Chris, too, took a step forward. Jude placed a hand on Chris's arm and said to the policeman, "Here he is. Here's your man."

The mob moved forward, but both police and thugs seemed curiously reluctant to touch Chris Davidson. Chris looked at them, almost amused, and spoke to the policeman behind the flashlight.

"All week I've been speaking in public, out in the open. If you had any cause to arrest me, why didn't you do it then? What were you so afraid of that you had to come at night, bringing a gang?"

John's voice spoke close to Pete's ear. "Don't run and don't try to fight. Let's just hang around and see what happens, then we'll know what we can do."

Pete and John followed the crowd at a slight distance, watching in horror as they forced Chris into the police car. Jude moved to get in beside him, but the cops pushed him away. "They don't need him anymore," John commented. Jude was squeezed into a rusted old car with some of the thugs; it was the one small moment of satisfaction Pete had all night.

Panic overtook him again as the cars pulled away. Glancing into John's eyes, he saw the reflection of his own uncertainty and fear.

"Look at the crowd," John said, stopping the van at the corner.

The city was still shrouded in predawn darkness, but a crowd had gathered outside the police station as Chris Davidson was brought in. Illuminated by the floodlights in the city hall square, they huddled on and around the steps, waiting. At first Pete had dared to hope that they were there to protest Chris's arrest, but their reaction as Chris was led up the steps told him clearly which side they were on.

"Right across the street from the hotel," John muttered, furious. "Just yesterday they couldn't get close enough to him. Now look at them. Scum!" He turned off the van's engine and looked at Pete. "I've got a buddy who's a janitor in there. Night shift. I bet he could let us in. You coming?"

Pete shook his head. He didn't want to go inside, near Chris; he didn't want to be a part of whatever horrible things were going to happen. He was Pete Johnson, an ordinary guy. Part of the crowd. If everything else was gone, that was what was left, and that was what he would be.

He moved through the crowd, not listening to their babble. When some woman elbowed him and said, "Hey! Do you know what's going on? Do you know Chris Davidson?" he kept his head down and ignored her till she turned her question elsewhere.

At the bottom of the steps he stopped, not wanting to push in any closer. To his dismay, he saw a reporter and cameraman elbowing through the crowd just in front of him. He looked away, hoping not to be recognized. But the reporter's sharp voice was aimed straight at him. "Excuse me, you're a follower of Mr. Davidson's, aren't you? Can you tell me how you—"

Pete recoiled from the microphone thrust in front of him. He shook his head and raised his hand in front of his face to cut out the glare of the camera's light. "No, sorry, I can't help you," he mumbled. "I don't know anything about it."

"But you are a friend of his, aren't you?" the young man persisted. Still shaking his head, Pete turned his back on the camera and edged away from the reporter, up the steps.

The crowd's movement jostled him, pushed him farther and farther up the steps till he was leaning against the railing near the door. The people were impatient, huddled together in the chilly, gray half-light. What were they waiting for?

A hand grasped his shoulder and pushed him forward; a camera was shoved in his face. "Here's one!" someone shouted. Pete looked up to see a young woman pointing the camera at him.

"Yes, that's right! You were with him! I saw you there when I covered the Castillo story!"

Pete hated her, hated the noisy people around him, hated his friends who had deserted him, hated Chris who had abandoned them, hated himself. This pushy girl with the fluffy red hair was the easiest person to hate, though, and Pete lashed out at her with the first words that came to his mind.

Then another voice cut in. "Sure he's one of that crowd. Can't you hear the Marselles accent?" Everyone laughed, and Pete swore again, then said, "Look, I'm telling you, I don't know the man. I don't know anything about this, now leave me alone!"

His very vehemence betrayed him, but the woman must have been an inexperienced reporter, because she didn't press her advantage. She turned away as the crowd stirred, craning their necks to see a pair of cops leading someone out the side door of the police station.

From his vantage point on the steps, Pete could look down at the man between the two officers. Handcuffed and guarded, he still walked with dignity. Then he turned to look up, behind him, and their eyes met.

Misery cut like a knife-edge through Pete. This was Chris Davidson—his boss, his best friend—looking at him with such pain and disappointment. Pete gripped the railing fiercely, wishing he could send Chris some signal of his loyalty. But the look on Chris's face told him he would know it was a lie. That look was the same as it had been when Chris had said, "You'll swear—three times—that you never knew me."

Pete bolted down the steps, tripping, running into people. He raced away from the crowd, from the square, down side streets and alleys. At last he stopped at the end of a deserted lane. He stumbled there, fell to his hands and knees, and stretched full length on the ground, his face pressed against the cold gravel.

Between the buildings, behind the hills that ringed the city, the first sunlight of day shot out, touching streets and cars and people, utterly missing the dark alley where an ordinary man lay sobbing bitterly on the ground.

Chapter Fifteen

Tall golden flowers bloomed all around in the grass at Maria's feet. She picked a few of them and added them to her bundle of daisies. The other women were going off to a florist's shop, but Maria had come here, to this field on the edge of town, to pick wildflowers. She hoped that when she placed them on Chris's grave, no one else would be there yet.

She couldn't stop remembering Friday afternoon. She sank to her knees in the dew-damp field, overcome by the pictures in her mind.

Everything about it was horrible. The almost savage hatred on the face of that unknown gunman. The smug complacency of the police who let him escape. They were there only to make sure that not too much attention was drawn to the affair. They had done nothing to stop the murder and would do nothing to punish it; they'd been in on the whole plan. She saw the faces of the knot of people around, the people who snapped pictures and video with their phones and gawked with curiosity at the man who'd been so controversial, now dead on the street.

She saw their faces, and she saw Chris's face. He had lain on the pavement for what seemed a long time before an ambulance finally came. He wasn't killed instantly by the bullet; Maria was there in time to see his last breaths, to watch the light leave his eyes. In those last seconds, Chris Davidson's face showed the simple agony of physical pain, and the hurt of someone betrayed. But there was something else there too—an anguish so intense that no physical or psychological torture on earth could account for it. It had echoed in his voice when he twisted his face to the sky and gasped out, "God—You've abandoned me! Why?"

No. Not that. She could feel that God had abandoned her, anyone on earth could feel that, but not him. The presence of God had been in and around Chris so clearly that it was impossible not to believe in God when he was there. If the Father whom Chris had spoken of had abandoned him, then either that God didn't exist, or else He hated the world.

That was what Maria had thought then, jostled on all sides by a screaming crowd, watching the man who had saved her life dying. She would still have thought it now, as she knelt weeping for him in a dark field, except for the one good picture to come out of that horrible Friday. Just before he finally died, Chris's features had cleared, and she saw again the traces of his perfect calm confidence. He looked as if everything was all right. But then he died, and everything was all wrong.

Maria stood up and brushed bits of damp grass from the knees of her jeans. The sun was rising. As she walked along, clutching her wildflowers, she saw a city bus in the distance. Automatically, she checked her pocket for change.

They were lucky, she supposed, to have a grave to visit at all. The reports of his death Friday night had been terse and said nothing about a funeral service. When a few of Chris's friends had found the courage to go to the police station on Saturday afternoon to make inquiries, they were told that there had been no autopsy and would be no inquest: Chris Davidson's body had already been buried quickly in the city cemetery, to avoid a "media circus."

Vale and Eastmount—the stop nearest the graveyard. She reached up to ring the bell and stood up as the bus lurched to a halt. The driver raised his hand in acknowledgment as she got off, and she waved back.

Despite the rumors she'd heard, there was no police car parked by the gate—no sign of anyone around at all, in fact. The just-risen sun threw grotesquely long shadows of the gate, the tombstones, and Maria over the green, dewy grass. Picking her way through shadows and sunlight, she found, finally, an unmarked grave that looked fresh and new, the earth recently turned over—just as Larry's had been, she remembered, that day when Chris had led them all to the Marselles graveyard and done the impossible.

When she got closer, Maria realized this couldn't be the right spot. This grave was open, freshly dug up as if waiting for a funeral later today. She looked to the right—there was the Whiting family monument with the enormous granite angel she had been told to use as a landmark. This had to be it, but—as she walked through the loose dirt to the edge of the grave, she recoiled in shock. This was not an empty grave waiting for a burial. There was something in there. A coffin, with its lid flung open. An empty coffin.

She stumbled away from the gaping hole and leaned against the Whitings' angel for support. Her flowers dropped, unheeded, to the ground. What had happened here? Something unthinkable—someone had opened the grave, taken his body! But why had they left the coffin? Couldn't the malicious, filthy creatures leave him alone even in death? What worse could they do to him now?

She ran from the graveyard, uncertain feet tripping in her haste. She was as anxious to get away from that strange place as she was to find her friends and tell them. Blindly, she pushed the gate open and raced down the street.

After a block, she slowed to a ragged walk. It was a long way; she couldn't hope to run the whole distance. This time no bus appeared. She half expected to get lost, so blindly was she walking. When she looked up and saw that she was at the far end of the street where the others were staying, she again broke into a run. She wanted desperately to be among friends.

Finally, she was there, pulling frantically at the door handle. It was locked. She pounded on the door and heard footsteps coming down the stairs toward her.

When John opened the door, she clutched at his arm. She gasped for a moment, trying to catch her breath, and then tried to tell him.

"What? Slow down, Maria. I don't understand."

She shook her head. "It's—the grave, his grave. It's empty. He's gone—"

"What?" John repeated. "Are you sure?"

It was a stupid question, but she didn't blame him. He had to say something while the news sank in. "Come and see," she urged.

"OK. Just a second." He ran up the stairs and looked into the room. "Maria's here—she's just been to the cemetery and she says the grave's been dug up or something. The body's gone. I'm going to go see. Does anyone—Pete, you want to come with me?"

There was a second of silence, then, "I guess so," said Pete.

As they drove along, John asked, "Did you see Audrey and the other women there?"

"No, they weren't there yet. Maybe they came after I left."

John strode ahead of Maria and Pete when they reached the cemetery. They found him at the edge of the open grave, looking down and frowning. He didn't look shocked, the way Maria had felt, but puzzled and almost intrigued. "This is weird," he told them. "Look at that dirt. It's not like it was dug up—it's scattered all over the place. And who would take the body and leave the coffin?"

Pete sat down on the low concrete wall. John looked at Maria, "I know, I wondered about that too," she said. "But then I thought . . . maybe they wanted to—to do something with it. I don't know—maybe they don't like him being buried here. You know, it's one of the biggest cemeteries in town, they probably don't think . . ."

John shook his head as her words trailed off. He ran a hand through his hair. "You know what this reminds me of?" he asked, still looking down. Pete looked up at him blankly, but Maria knew.

"Larry's grave," she said, though she hadn't meant to speak.

John nodded, a half smile on his long, slender young face. "Remember what everyone said on Friday, when Chris was arrested? 'He's supposed to have raised the dead, but he can't save himself.'" His eyes met Maria's, and she saw that they were radiant with hope. "Kind of makes you think, doesn't it?"

"No!" Pete jumped to his feet and grabbed John's arm. "No, John, don't try to fool yourself into believing that. Whatever else happens, Chris is dead. You've got to accept that."

John shrugged. "Well," he said, "let's go back and see what the others think." As he turned to go, Maria could see that already he looked stronger, more hopeful, than when he had come. Pete, just a few steps away, seemed to be standing in shadow.

"Coming, Maria?" John asked.

She shook her head. "No, I want to stay here for a while. I'll walk back later."

She heard the gates creak shut again and heard the van drive away. She knelt in the grass and dirt, picking up the scattered flowers. Her heart wanted to fly at the thought of what John believed—what John wanted to believe—but she knew Pete was right. It wasn't safe to hope. Her tears began again—tears for Chris, for the hope he had given her and for the loss of that hope.

Maria heard someone come up behind her. She didn't turn around, even when a voice said, "Are you all right? Who are you looking for?"

The voice was kind, so it couldn't be a cop—the caretaker, perhaps? She didn't even notice at first that his second question was a rather strange one. She answered it, though she still didn't turn around. Whoever this man was, he must know whose grave had been here. "Sir, if you know where he is, if you've taken him, please tell me. I'll pay whatever it costs—we could have him buried back in Marselles, where his friends are—"

"Maria."

Her name—his voice! The first word that voice had ever said to me! She half rose, turning quickly, and fell back on her knees again. As she had also done the first time, for here again was God, whom she must worship.

"Oh, my Lord!" The words sprang from her in a burst of joy. She thought how kind it was for him to meet her here, knowing how wretched she was. But her mind wasn't on those thoughts: it was on him. He stood with his back to the morning sun, but instead of looking silhouetted against that light, he seemed to shine in it. It was the same familiar form, the same confident pose, though he was dressed not in the familiar jeans and T-shirt but in a suit of some light-catching material, far finer than anything she had seen him wear before. And, of course, his face was the same—those eyes and that smile could belong to no one else. Yet, too, there was something different. His face was as strong and clear as if it were a sculpture; the lines of weariness that she had remembered had been polished from it. And he, who had always been so full of life, glowed with new vitality. Everything about him seemed more vivid—it was as if she were looking at a living human being for the first time.

She knelt at his feet, gazing up in worship, taking in all the details. He was back. He was the God of all the universe, and he was looking at her as though seeing her again was his greatest joy.

"Go to the others," he said at last. "To my brothers," and as he called them that, the same pleasure flashed again in his eyes, and she knew how eager he must be to end their suffering. "Tell them I'm going to see my Father, who is their Father, too, and to my God, who is their God." Then, with a last smile, he turned to walk away. She looked back down at the ground, and up again, and, as she had expected, he was not there.

But he had been real. And she had to go find the others, to tell them.

Chapter Sixteen

The lake was completely flat with an eerie predawn calm. Pete leaned on the rail, staring out at it. "It's good to be up here again," Andy said.

"Yeah. Not the same without Chris, though."

"Oh, he'll be up here. He told us he'd meet us up here." They had spoken with Chris twice now, back in the city, since the women had reported that he was—incredibly—alive that Sunday morning.

The Fisher boys had come out of the lodge and joined them on the deck while Pete was speaking. The four men walked down to the boathouse. "What really amazes me," John said as they pulled the largest of the boats out into the water, "is that now that Chris has come back to life, we know he really is God. And that means—God is someone we hung around with. Someone who helped us fix the van and cook a meal and buy the groceries. He understands us. That blows my mind." Three more shadowy figures emerged through the trees and out onto the dock.

"We woke up early and thought we'd join you guys," Nat said. Phil was behind him and, somewhat to Pete's surprise, so was Tomas, who had seemed different ever since he'd seen Chris back in the city. Well, they were all different, weren't they?

The boat was soon loaded and sped away from shore. When they were well out on the lake, Pete cut the motor and got busy preparing bait and tackle like everyone else. This early morning fishing trip had been his idea—a release of tension, but also a necessity, since so many people were staying in the lodge and there was no surplus of either food or money. They'd been up here all week, waiting for Chris to come or something to happen. Pete and Andy had taken on a job fixing a truck for someone in town. Pete couldn't stand being idle, and someone had to bring in a little cash. That job was finished now, and a few big bass wouldn't go astray at the crowded breakfast table.

Luck, though, seemed to be against them. They fished in silence, and the water remained as calm as glass, but no fish were biting. More than an hour slipped by. Dawn streaked the sky rose and gold, and the sun slipped through the trees on the eastern ridge.

The boat had drifted closer to shore. Looking up, Pete noticed a man standing on the shore. He thought he saw a movement—was the man waving at them? Then, clear across the water, a voice called out, "Catch anything, boys?"

"Not a thing," Pete called back to the friendly stranger.

"Try casting off on the other side!"

Pete rolled his eyes and looked at the others—then he caught John's glance. Wordlessly, Pete reeled in his empty line and cast off on the other side—not that he hadn't tried over there before. The others began to do likewise, but even before John had his line in the water, Pete felt a tug. He looked at John and they both nodded.

"It's him, all right," said John, grinning.

Pete dropped his fishing rod without even bothering to reel

in the line—there were plenty more fish out there, no doubt. In a single movement, he jumped from the boat into the chilly water. "Hey, watch out!" yelled Jim as the boat rocked dangerously.

His feet scraped bottom, and he splashed onto the shore. He was close enough now to see that it was really Chris on the beach—though as always since his resurrection, you couldn't be sure just by looking. The face and form were familiar, but also changed—fired by the same glory Pete had seen once on a hilltop. But that smile, and the handclasp that helped him out of the water, could not belong to anyone else.

From the boat came the shouts of the other men as they reeled in one big fish after another. Pete noticed a fire burning on the beach with some fish already cleaned and frying on it. He decided not to ask where the fish had come from—or for that matter what Chris was doing on the far side of the lake without a boat.

Pete listened to the voices of Chris and the others as they sat around the fire sharing their simple meal. Early morning loons cried far out on the lake, and sparks snapped on the fire. He had traveled a long way from Pete's Garage to this fireside, and he had a feeling there was a long way yet to go, but he knew in this moment that he'd found whatever it was he'd set out looking for.

After the food was gone, Andy and Phil set to work putting out the fire, and the others drifted back toward the boat. Pete found himself walking up the beach with Chris. They hadn't talked one-on-one since their brief encounter on the day Chris had come back to life. That day, Chris had said all Pete needed to know to be sure that he was forgiven. Still, it felt funny to be alone with him.

"Rocky?" That name called back so many memories.

"Yes?"

"Do you love me—more than everything else?" Chris's

gesture took in the beach and the boat and Pete's friends and the lodge where Audrey and the kids were waking to a new day. All the same, it was an easy question.

"Yes, boss. I do love you."

"Do you really, Pete?"

He thought then of their last conversation before Chris's death, of the pain and concern in Chris's eyes. He heard his own voice saying, "Look, I'm telling you, I don't know the man!" He felt again the cold gravel of a deserted alley against his face and saw the tortured death he had not been brave enough to watch. "You know I love you, boss."

"Then care for my children, Pete—my little ones." He was placing a responsibility on Pete's shoulders. Pretty ironic now that Pete had finally proven himself unworthy of the kind of leadership he'd always wanted. But knowing Chris, this was what he was waiting for all along—for Pete Johnson to fall off his pedestal.

"Right," said Chris, placing a hand on Pete's shoulder as if he'd spoken those thoughts aloud. "You're ready for it now."

Only then did Pete think of the other implication of those words. "You're going away again, aren't you?" he asked reluctantly.

Chris Davidson nodded. They walked on. "I do have to go away—I told you that, but I told you I'd come back, too. Remember?"

"I remember." Pete thought of the house with many rooms—a room in it for everyone. "But I can't imagine life without you. Can we get by without you?"

"You won't have to. I promised I'd send my Spirit—haven't you found that out by now?"

Pete remembered the feeling they'd all talked about—that Chris was there even when he wasn't. "You mean—"

Again, Chris nodded. "After I've gone back to my Father, you'll be even more aware of that Spirit."

"It still won't be quite the same," Pete said. "But that'll give me something to look forward to."

They turned back to walk toward the boat and the others. A few minutes later, they were all in the boat—Chris with them, this time—and heading back to the lodge.

"So he's not going to disappear this time?" Andy asked quietly, below the roar of the motor.

"Not just yet," Pete replied. "He's got to go away, but I think he's going to spend a little time with us first. There's probably a lot of stuff he needs to say to everybody."

"Good," said Andy, keeping his eyes on the water.

Pete, too, watched the lake as the boat sped across to the other shore. The sun glinted off every blue ripple in the water, the morning wind cut fresh and clean across his face, and gulls cried overhead. He wished there were some way to make the boat go faster. He couldn't wait to get back and tell Audrey about—well, everything.